THE GREAT GATSBY

On a warm summer night in 1922, Jay Gatsby stands in the garden of his mansion on Long Island, looking out across the dark water of the bay. Out at sea is a green light, tiny and far away, and Gatsby stretches out his arms toward this light, trembling a little.

Newly arrived in Long Island, Nick Carraway watches Gatsby from his garden next door, and wonders. Who is this mysterious Jay Gatsby, whose generous champagne parties are famous all over New York? Where did his great wealth come from? The beautiful people who drink and dance all night at his parties are full of wild tales about Gatsby's past – is he a murderer, is he a bootlegger? – but nobody knows the answers.

At a dinner party with Tom and Daisy Buchanan, Nick meets Jordan Baker, and is soon drawn into the life of Long Island. And as the summer passes, he slowly begins to uncover the mystery that is Jay Gatsby.

It is a story of excitement and violence, of love and despair; a story of bright, romantic hopes and impossible, hopeless dreams . . .

OXFORD BOOKWORMS LIBRARY
Classics

The Great Gatsby

Stage 5 (1800 headwords)

Series Editor: Jennifer Bassett
Founder Editor: Tricia Hedge
Activities Editors: Jennifer Bassett and Christine Lindop

Then wear the gold hat, if that will move her;
    If you can bounce high, bounce for her too,
Till she cry "Lover, gold-hatted, high-bouncing lover,
    I must have you!"
                        THOMAS PARKE D'INVILLIERS

F. SCOTT FITZGERALD

The Great Gatsby

Retold by
Clare West

OXFORD UNIVERSITY PRESS

OXFORD
UNIVERSITY PRESS

Great Clarendon Street, Oxford, OX2 6DP, United Kingdom

Oxford University Press is a department of the University of Oxford.
It furthers the University's objective of excellence in research, scholarship,
and education by publishing worldwide. Oxford is a registered trade
mark of Oxford University Press in the UK and in certain other countries

This simplified edition © Oxford University Press 2013

The moral rights of the author have been asserted

First published in Oxford Bookworms 2013

28

No unauthorized photocopying

All rights reserved. No part of this publication may be reproduced,
stored in a retrieval system, or transmitted, in any form or by any means,
without the prior permission in writing of Oxford University Press, or as
expressly permitted by law, by licence or under terms agreed with the
appropriate reprographics rights organization. Enquiries concerning
reproduction outside the scope of the above should be sent to the ELT
Rights Department, Oxford University Press, at the address above

You must not circulate this work in any other form and you must
impose this same condition on any acquirer

Links to third party websites are provided by Oxford in good faith and
for information only. Oxford disclaims any responsibility for the materials
contained in any third party website referenced in this work

ISBN: 978 0 19 478617 1   Book
ISBN: 978 0 19 462116 8   Book and audio pack

Printed in China

Word count (main text): 23,445 words

For more information on the Oxford Bookworms Library,
visit www.oup.com/elt/gradedreaders

ACKNOWLEDGEMENTS

Text adapted by Clare West

Illustrated by Gavin Reece

Cover image Portrait of Paul Cadmus, 1928 (oil on canvas), by Luigi Lucioni (1900–1988)
Brooklyn Museum of Art, New York, USA/Dick S Ramsay Fund/Bridgeman Images

Despite their best efforts, the Publishers have been unable to trace the
copyright holder of the cover image, but would be pleased to hear
from the copyright holder if they would like to contact them.

The publishers would like to thank the following for their permission to reproduce images:
Alamy p. 100 (Edwin Remsberg).

CONTENTS

	INTRODUCTION	i
	PEOPLE IN THIS STORY	viii
	PLACE NAMES IN THIS STORY	viii
1	Dinner with the Buchanans	1
2	Meeting Tom's mistress	11
3	A party at Gatsby's	20
4	Gatsby's past	28
5	Gatsby and Daisy meet again	37
6	The truth about Gatsby	46
7	A hot day in town	55
8	Wilson's revenge	72
9	The funeral	81
	GLOSSARY	90
	ACTIVITIES: Before Reading	93
	ACTIVITIES: While Reading	94
	ACTIVITIES: After Reading	96
	ABOUT THE AUTHOR	99
	ABOUT THE BOOKWORMS LIBRARY	101

PEOPLE IN THIS STORY

MAIN CHARACTERS
Nick Carraway, *the narrator of the story*
Jay Gatsby (*also* James Gatz), *a young mysterious millionaire*
Daisy Buchanan, *distant cousin to Nick Carraway*
Tom Buchanan, *Daisy's husband, a millionaire*
Jordan Baker, *Daisy's friend, a young professional female golfer*
Myrtle Wilson, *Tom Buchanan's mistress*
George Wilson, *Myrtle's husband, a garage owner*

OTHER CHARACTERS
Meyer Wolfshiem, *a gambler, a business connection of Gatsby*
Catherine, *Myrtle Wilson's sister*
Mr & Mrs McKee, *Myrtle Wilson's New York friends*
Klipspringer, *a man who is almost always at Gatsby's house*
Michaelis, *George Wilson's neighbor*
Henry C. Gatz, *Jay Gatsby's father*

PLACE NAMES IN THIS STORY

Some place names in the story are real; others are invented. The story is set on Long Island, which stretches for more than 100 miles east of New York City. *West Egg* in the story is Great Neck (where Scott Fitzgerald himself lived), and *East Egg* is Sands Point, the end of the Port Washington peninsula, which lies just across Manhasset Bay.

In the story *the East* refers to the east coast of the United States, and *the West* to the west coast. The *Middle West*, or *Mid-West*, includes states like Minnesota and cities like Chicago. However, anybody who was not from the east coast might be called a *Westerner*.

CHAPTER 1

DINNER WITH THE BUCHANANS

In my younger and more vulnerable years my father gave me some advice that I've been turning over in my mind ever since.

'Whenever you feel like judging anyone,' he told me, 'just remember that all the people in this world haven't had the advantages that you've had.'

He didn't say any more, but I understood that he meant a great deal more than that. As a result, I usually wait some time before making any judgements. This habit has opened up many strange characters to me, as people are often eager to tell me about themselves. When I was at college, I was unjustly accused of being a politician, because I knew the secret sadnesses of wild, unknown men. I hardly ever wanted to hear these secrets – in fact, I have often pretended to be asleep or busy when I realized by some unmistakable sign that a young man was preparing to tell me his deepest, most personal feelings.

Holding back judgement is a matter of hope. There is always the possibility that someone, in time, will turn out well. What my father was suggesting was that we are all born with a different sense of right and wrong. And if I forget that, then I am a little afraid of missing something.

However, I have to confess that I haven't always taken my father's advice. When I came back from the East last autumn, I felt I wanted the whole world to be in moral uniform, all living a highly moral life for ever. I wanted no more wildness, no more secrets of the human heart. Only Gatsby, the man who gives his name to this book, was an exception – Gatsby, who represented everything for which I would normally have only the deepest scorn. There was something truly wonderful about him, a heightened sensitivity to the promises of life – he was like one of those complicated machines that show the presence of an earthquake ten thousand miles away. He had an extraordinary gift for hope, a romantic readiness which I have never found in any other person and which it is not likely I shall ever find again. No – Gatsby turned out all right at the end. It was what lay in wait for Gatsby, what foul dust followed on the heels of his dreams that, for a while, ended my interest in the failed sorrows and short-lived joys of men.

• —— •

My family, the Carraways, have been successful, fairly wealthy people in this Middle Western city for many years. My grandfather's brother came here in 1851 and started the business that my father carries on today. I finished my studies at Yale University in 1915, and a little later I took part in the Great War. I enjoyed this excursion so much that I came back from Europe feeling restless. Instead of being the warm center of the world, the Middle West now seemed like the torn edge of it. So I decided to go East, to New York, and learn the bond business. Everybody I knew was in the bond business, so I supposed it could support one more single man. All my aunts and uncles talked it over and finally said, 'Why – ye-es,' with very serious, hesitant faces. Father agreed to pay me an income for a year, and I came East, for ever, I thought, in the spring of 1922.

The sensible thing was to find rooms in the city, but it was a warm season and I had just left a country of wide lawns and friendly trees. So when a young man at the office suggested we should rent a house together just outside the city, it sounded like a great idea. He found the house, a small weather-beaten place at eighty dollars a month, but at the last minute the company ordered him to move to Washington, and I went out to the country alone. I had a dog – at least I had him for a few days until he ran away – and an old car, and a woman from Finland, who made my bed and cooked breakfast and whispered darkly to herself in Finnish in the kitchen.

It was lonely for a day or so, until one morning some man, more recently arrived than I, stopped me on the road.

'How do you get to West Egg village?' he asked helplessly.

I told him. And as I walked on, I was lonely no longer. I was a guide, a pathfinder. I belonged to the place. Without knowing it, he had given me the freedom of the neighborhood.

And so, with the sunshine, and the leaves bursting out on the trees, I had that recognizable feeling that life was beginning over again with the summer.

My house was on that slender island which lies east of New York. At one end of the island the land is in the shape of two enormous eggs, separated by a bay. They look so similar that they must be confusing for the seabirds that fly over them. But the wingless on the ground know that they are dissimilar in everything except shape and size.

East Egg was the more fashionable of the two, where the rich lived in unbelievable luxury. I lived at West Egg, where most people were managing on comparatively low incomes. Surprisingly, the house next to mine was an enormous place – it was an exact copy of some grand Town Hall in France, with a tower on one side, a beautiful swimming pool, and extremely large gardens. It was Gatsby's mansion, although, as I didn't know him then, to me it was simply a mansion inhabited by someone of that name. My own house was small and ugly, but

I had a view of the water, a part view of my neighbor's lawn, and the comfortable feeling of living close to millionaires – all for eighty dollars a month.

Across the bay the white palaces of East Egg shone along the water, and the history of the summer really begins on the evening I drove over there to have dinner with the Buchanans. Daisy was a distant cousin of mine, and I'd known her husband Tom in college; they had a very young daughter, whom I'd never met.

Tom had been one of the strongest players in the Yale football team. He was one of those men who reach such limited excellence at twenty-one that everything afterwards is a little disappointing. His family were enormously wealthy. He and Daisy had spent a year in France for no particular reason, and then moved here and there, unrestfully, wherever people rode horses and were rich together.

And so it happened that on a warm windy evening I drove over to East Egg to see two old friends whom I didn't know at all well. Their house was even larger than I expected, a cheerful red-and-white mansion overlooking the bay. The windows were wide open to the sun and wind, and Tom Buchanan in riding clothes was standing with his legs apart on the front porch.

He had changed since his years at Yale. Now he was a well-built man of thirty, with a rather hard mouth and a proud manner. Not even his beautifully made riding clothes could hide his body's enormous power – you could see the muscles moving under his thin coat. It was a cruel body, capable of anything.

He greeted me and took me into a bright rosy-colored room. A light wind blew through it, blowing curtains in and out like pale flags at the windows. In the center of the room was a large sofa, on which two women were lying. They were both in long white dresses, which were rising and falling with the wind, until Tom banged shut the windows.

From her sofa Daisy turned to me and held my hand for a moment. She gave a pretty little laugh and looked up into my

Daisy turned to me and held my hand for a moment.

face, promising that there was no one in the world she so much wanted to see. That was a way she had. She mentioned that the other girl's name was Baker, and Miss Baker and I greeted each other politely.

Daisy asked me questions in her low, exciting voice. Her face was sad and lovely, with bright eyes and a bright beautiful mouth, but it was her voice that men who loved her found difficult to forget. It had a singing kind of power, a whispered 'Listen', a promise that she had done amusing, exciting things just a while ago and that there were amusing, exciting things to do in the next hour.

The butler brought in four drinks, but Miss Baker said, 'No, thanks, I'm absolutely in training.'

I looked at her, wondering what she was in training for. I enjoyed looking at her. She was a slender, small-breasted girl who held herself very straight, and she had gray eyes in a pale, pretty, frowning face.

'You live in West Egg,' she remarked scornfully. 'I know somebody there.'

'I don't know a single—'

'You must know Gatsby.'

'Gatsby?' demanded Daisy. 'What Gatsby?'

'Dinner is served, madam,' the butler said, before I could reply, and we all went to sit down at a table on a porch outside.

'Look!' said Daisy suddenly. Her eyes were on her little finger. We all looked. It was black and blue.

'You did it, Tom,' she said accusingly. 'I know you didn't mean to, but you *did* do it. That's what I get for marrying a great big powerful animal of a man.'

'I hate that word animal,' said Tom crossly, 'even as a joke.'

'Animal,' insisted Daisy.

We talked of this and that through dinner. Daisy and Miss Baker made polite, pleasant conversation that was as cool as their white dresses. Tom seemed restless. Inside the house the telephone rang, and the butler came to whisper in Tom's ear. Tom frowned and without a word went inside. Daisy bent forward and spoke to me.

'I love to see you at my table, Nick. You remind me of – of a rose, an absolute rose. Doesn't he?' She turned to Miss Baker.

This was untrue. I am nothing like a rose. I felt that her heart was trying to come out to me, hidden in those breathless, warm words. Then suddenly she got up and went into the house.

I was about to speak when Miss Baker said 'Shh!' in a warning voice. She bent forward to listen unashamedly to the low voice we could hear inside the house.

'This Mr Gatsby you spoke of is my neighbor—' I began.

'Don't talk. I want to hear what happens.'

'Is something happening?' I asked innocently.

'You mean to say you don't know?' said Miss Baker, honestly surprised. 'I thought everybody knew.' She hesitated for a moment. 'Tom's got some woman in New York.'

Almost before I had understood what she meant, Tom and Daisy were back at the table.

'It couldn't be helped!' cried Daisy brightly. Her voice shook a little as she continued, 'There's a beautiful bird singing in the garden. It's romantic, isn't it, Tom?'

'Very romantic,' he said, and then miserably to me, 'If it's light enough after dinner, I want to show you my horses.'

The telephone rang inside again, and as Daisy shook her head decisively at Tom, there was no further conversation of any kind and the dinner came to an end. Tom and Miss Baker went into the library, while I followed Daisy round the outside of the house to the front porch. In the darkness we sat down on a long seat.

Daisy took her lovely face in her hands. I saw that powerful feelings had taken hold of her, so I asked what I hoped would be some calming questions about her little girl.

'We don't know each other very well, Nick,' she said suddenly. 'You didn't come to my wedding.'

'I wasn't back from the war.'

'That's true.' She hesitated. 'Well, I've had a very bad time, Nick, and I don't believe in anyone or anything any more.'

I waited but she didn't say any more, and after a moment I returned rather weakly to asking about her daughter.

'I suppose she talks, and – eats, and everything.'

'Oh, yes.' She looked at me absently. 'Listen, Nick, let me tell you what I said when she was born. Would you like to hear?'

'Very much.'

'Well, she was less than an hour old, and Tom was God knows where. I woke up, feeling completely alone, and asked the nurse if it was a boy or a girl. She told me it was a girl, and so I turned my head away and cried. "I'm glad it's a girl," I said. "And I hope she'll be a fool – that's the best thing a girl can be in this world, a beautiful little fool."

'You see, I think everything's terrible anyway. Everybody thinks so. And I *know*. I've been everywhere and seen everything and done everything. Nothing's new to *me!*' She laughed scornfully.

The moment her voice stopped, her power over me died away. I felt the basic insincerity of what she had said, and it made me uneasy. I waited, and sure enough, a second later she looked at me with a silly smile on her lovely face.

Inside, the red-colored room was full of light. Miss Baker

was reading aloud to Tom from the *Saturday Evening Post*. As we entered, she stood up.

'Ten o'clock,' she said. 'Time for this good girl to go to bed.'

'Jordan's playing in an important match tomorrow,' Daisy explained.

Suddenly I knew who she was – Jordan Baker, the well-known golfer. Photos of her were in all the sports magazines. I had heard some story about her too, an unpleasant one, but I couldn't quite remember it.

We all said goodnight, and she went upstairs.

'She's a nice girl,' said Tom after a moment. 'Her family oughtn't to let her run around the country this way.'

'Her family is one aunt about a thousand years old,' said Daisy coldly. 'Anyway, Nick's going to look after her, aren't you, Nick? She's going to spend lots of weekends out here this summer. I think the home influence will be very good for her.'

Daisy and Tom looked at each other for a moment in silence.

'Did you give Nick a little heart-to-heart talk on the porch?' demanded Tom suddenly.

'Did I?' She looked at me. 'I can't seem to remember.'

'Don't believe everything you hear, Nick,' he advised me.

'Oh, I heard nothing at all,' I said lightly.

A little later I got up to go home. They came to the door with me and stood side by side in a cheerful square of light.

'Wait!' called Daisy. 'I forgot to ask – we heard you were engaged to a girl out West.'

'That's right,' agreed Tom. 'We heard that.'

'It's not true. I'm too poor to get engaged.' Of course I knew what they were talking about. It was one of the reasons I had come East. The girl was an old friend, but people had started saying we were engaged, and I had no intention of marrying.

Their interest rather touched me, but I was still confused as I drove away. It seemed to me that the thing for Daisy to do was to rush out of the house, child in arms – but she did not appear to have any such intentions in her head. As for Tom, the fact that he 'had some woman in New York' was not at all surprising.

Already it was deep summer, and when I reached my house, I put the car away and sat for a while out in my small garden. It was a loud, bright night, with wings beating in the trees and insects flying above my head. A cat moved across the grass in the moonlight, and, turning my head to watch it, I saw that I was not alone. A figure had appeared from the shadow of my neighbor's mansion and was standing with his hands in his pockets, looking up at the silver stars. Something about him suggested it was Mr Gatsby himself, who had come out to determine what share of our local sky was his.

I was going to call to him, but his next action suggested that he wanted to be alone. He stretched out his arms toward the dark water in a rather strange way, and although I was some distance from him, I felt sure he was trembling. I too looked out to sea – and saw nothing except a green light, tiny and far away. When I looked once more for Gatsby, he had disappeared, and I was alone again in the unquiet darkness.

CHAPTER 2

MEETING TOM'S MISTRESS

Halfway between West Egg and New York, the road meets the railway and runs next to it for a quarter of a mile, in order to avoid a certain unpleasant area of land. This is a valley of ashes – a fantastic farm where ashes grow into hills and strange-looking gardens, where they take the shape of houses and chimneys, and finally of ash-gray men. Occasionally a line of gray cars moves slowly along an invisible path and comes to rest, and immediately the ash-gray men rush up and start digging, creating a thick cloud of gray dust all around them.

But after a moment, above the gray land and through the dust clouds, you see the eyes of Doctor T. J. Eckleburg. They are blue and enormous, and look out of no face, but instead from a pair of huge yellow glasses. The advertisement must have been put up there by some local eye specialist, who then forgot it and moved away. But the eyes, paler now after many paintless days under sun and rain, still look thoughtfully out over the rubbish heaps.

On one side of the valley is a small, dirty river, where trains always have to stop for at least a minute before crossing. It was because of this that I first met Tom Buchanan's mistress.

Everyone knew that he had one. Although I was curious about her, I had no particular wish to meet her. I went up to New York with Tom on the train one afternoon, and when we stopped by the ash-heaps, he jumped to his feet and, taking hold of my elbow, forced me to get off the train.

'We're getting off,' he insisted. 'I want you to meet my girl.'

I had the feeling he'd drunk a good deal at lunch. He must

have thought I had nothing better to do on a Sunday afternoon, which rather annoyed me.

We got off the train and walked back along the road under Doctor Eckleburg's staring eyes. It was like a desert around us. There was only one small building standing on its own on the edge of the ash-heaps. It contained three shops. One was for rent, and another was an all-night restaurant; the third was a garage, with a sign saying *Repairs GEORGE B. WILSON Cars bought and sold*. I followed Tom inside.

The garage looked unused and almost empty. The only car visible was a dust-covered old Ford in a dark corner. I thought this shadow of a garage must be a pretence, and that luxurious, romantic apartments must be hidden upstairs. Then the owner himself appeared at the door of an office. He was a fair-haired, dull-looking man, pale, and almost handsome. When he saw us, a hopeful look came into his light blue eyes.

'Hello, Wilson,' said Tom cheerfully. 'How's business?'

'I can't complain,' answered Wilson doubtfully. 'When are you going to sell me that car?'

'Next week. I've got my man working on it now.'

'Works pretty slow, don't he?'

'No, he doesn't,' said Tom coldly. 'And if you feel that way about it, maybe I'd better sell it to someone else.'

'I don't mean that,' explained Wilson quickly. ' I just—'

His voice died away and Tom looked impatiently around the garage. I heard footsteps on the stairs, and in a moment the thickish figure of a woman darkened the office doorway. She was in her mid-thirties, and heavily-built, but carried herself sensuously. There was nothing of beauty in her face, but she had an immediately noticeable vitality – her whole body seemed to be giving off waves of heat. She smiled slowly and, walking past her ghost-like husband, shook hands with Tom, looking him full in the face. Then she ran her tongue around her lips, and, without turning to look at Wilson, spoke to him in a soft, coarse voice.

'Get some chairs, why don't you, so somebody can sit down.'

Wilson hurried back to the little office. A white ashen dust covered his dark suit and everything around him – except his wife. She moved close to Tom.

'I want to see you,' said Tom quietly. 'Get on the next train.'

'All right,' said Mrs Wilson. She moved away from Tom just as George Wilson came out of his office with two chairs.

We waited for her down the road, out of sight. A thin, gray-looking child was playing near the ash-heaps by the road.

'Terrible place, isn't it,' said Tom, frowning at Doctor Eckleburg.

'Awful.'

'It does her good to get away.'

'Doesn't her husband ask questions?'

'Wilson? He thinks she goes to see her sister in New York. He's so dumb he doesn't know he's alive.'

So Tom Buchanan and his girl and I went up together to New York – or not quite together, because Mrs Wilson sat separately from us, in case there were other East Eggers on the train.

When we got out of the train, Mrs Wilson bought two magazines and a bottle of perfume at the station shop. Then she noticed an old man with a basket of little dogs for sale, and told Tom she wanted one. Tom was not enthusiastic, but handed over some money and Mrs Wilson chose her dog. In the taxi she held it delightedly in her arms.

We arrived at Tom's apartment on 158th Street, and I made an attempt to say goodbye. But Tom wanted me to come up to the apartment, and Mrs Wilson said she would telephone her sister Catherine to join us, so I went up with them.

The apartment was on the top floor – a small living room, a small dining room, a small bedroom, and a bath. It was crowded with furniture that was much too large for it. Tom brought out a bottle of whisky from a locked cupboard.

I have been drunk just twice in my life, and the second time was that afternoon, so everything that happened has a misty quality about it. Sitting on Tom's knees Mrs Wilson called up several people on the phone, then I went out to buy cigarettes. When I came back, they had both disappeared, so I politely sat down and waited in the living room. Just as Tom and Myrtle reappeared (after the first drink Mrs Wilson and I called each other by our first names), guests started arriving.

The sister, Catherine, was a slender, worldly girl of about thirty, with red hair. There was also a man called Chester McKee, from the flat below. He had just shaved, and there was still a tiny bit of shaving soap on his face. I learnt that he was a photographer. His wife was loud, slow, handsome, and horrible. She told me proudly that her husband had photographed her one hundred and twenty-seven times since they had been married.

Mrs Wilson had changed her clothes and was wearing an expensive afternoon dress. With the influence of the dress, her character had also changed. The warm vitality that had been so remarkable in the garage had become overpowering arrogance.

'My dear,' she told her sister loudly, 'most of these servants will cheat you every time. All they think of is money.'

'I like your dress,' remarked Mrs McKee, 'it's wonderful.'

Mrs Wilson looked scornful. 'This crazy old thing? I just slip it on sometimes when I don't care what I look like.'

'If Chester could only get you, in that position,' continued Mrs McKee, 'I think he could make something of it.'

We all stared in silence at Mrs Wilson, who pushed back her hair from her eyes and looked back at us with her brightest smile. Mr McKee looked at her carefully, his head on one side.

'I'd change the light,' he said after a moment.

'I wouldn't think of changing the light–' cried Mrs McKee.

'Shh!' said her husband, deep in artistic thought, and we all looked at Myrtle again. Suddenly Tom yawned and stood up.

'You McKees, have something to drink,' he said. 'Get some more ice, Myrtle, before everybody goes to sleep.'

'I *told* that boy about the ice.' Myrtle rolled her eyes upwards. 'These people! You have to keep an eye on them all the time.' She looked at me and laughed pointlessly. Then she marched purposefully into the kitchen, clearly wanting us to think she had ten hired cooks in there, waiting for her orders.

Her sister, Catherine, sat down beside me on the sofa.

'Do you live down on Long Island, too?' she asked.

'I live at West Egg.'

'Really? I was down there at a party about a month ago. At Gatsby's. Do you know him?'

'I live next door to him.'

'Well, they say he's a relation of Kaiser Wilhelm's. That's where all his money comes from – the German royal family.'

'Really?' I was interested.

'I'm afraid of him. I'd hate him to know anything about me.'

She looked over at Tom and Myrtle, then whispered, 'Neither of them can *stand* the person they're married to.'

'Can't they?'

'Get some more ice, Myrtle, before everybody goes to sleep.'

'Can't *stand* them. What I say is, why go on living with them if they can't stand them? If I was them, I'd get a divorce and get married to each other as soon as possible.'

'Doesn't your sister like her husband, then?'

The answer to this was unexpected. It came from Myrtle, who had overheard the question, and it was violent and rude.

'You see!' cried Catherine, pleased that she was right. She went on in a lower voice, 'It's really Tom's wife that's keeping them apart. She doesn't believe in divorce.'

I knew this wasn't true, and I was a little shocked at the lie.

Suddenly we heard the sharp, high voice of Mrs McKee across the room. 'I almost married the wrong man,' she was saying to Myrtle. 'I knew he was far below me socially. But if I hadn't met Chester, the nasty little man would have got me, that's for sure.'

'But at least you *didn't* marry the wrong man,' said Myrtle. 'The difference between you and me is that I *did*.'

'Why *did* you marry George, Myrtle?' demanded Catherine.

'I thought he knew how to behave to a lady, but he was no good. I wouldn't let him lick my shoe.'

'You were crazy about him for a while,' said Catherine.

'Crazy about him!' cried Myrtle in horror. 'I never was any more crazy about him than I was about that man there.'

She pointed suddenly at me, and everyone looked at me accusingly. I tried to show by my expression that I didn't expect to be loved.

'She really ought to get away from him,' Catherine whispered to me. 'They've been living over that garage for eleven years. And Tom's the first boyfriend she ever had.'

A second bottle of whisky was now constantly in demand by all present, except Catherine, who 'felt just as good on nothing at all'. I wanted to get out and walk eastward toward the park in the soft evening half-light, but each time I tried to go, I got involved in some wild argument, which pulled me back into the room. Anyone watching in the darkening streets outside must have seen our yellow windows high up against the sky, and I was that person too, looking up and wondering. I was inside and outside, at the same time delighted and horrified by the never-ending variety of life.

Myrtle brought her chair close to mine, and her warm breath poured over me the story of her first meeting with Tom.

'I was going up to New York to see my sister and spend the night. Tom sat opposite me on the train, and I couldn't take my eyes off him. When we came into the station, he was next to me, and his shirt-front was touching my arm, so I told him I'd have to call a policeman, but he knew I was lying. I was so excited when I got into a taxi with him that I didn't really know where I was. All I kept thinking about, over and over, was "You can't live forever, you can't live forever".'

She turned to Mrs McKee and the room rang full of her false laughter.

'My dear,' she cried, 'I'm giving you this dress as soon as I've finished with it. I've got to buy another one tomorrow. I'm going to make a list of all the things I'm going to buy.'

It was nine o'clock – almost immediately afterwards I looked at my watch and found it was ten. Mr McKee was asleep in a chair. Taking out my handkerchief, I removed from his face the dried shaving soap that had worried me all the afternoon.

People disappeared, reappeared, made plans to go somewhere, and then lost each other, searched for each other, found each other nearby.

Some time around midnight, Tom and Mrs Wilson stood

face to face, discussing in loud angry voices whether Mrs Wilson was allowed to mention Daisy's name.

'Daisy! Daisy! Daisy!' shouted Mrs Wilson. 'I'll say it whenever I want to! Daisy! Dai—'

With a short, deliberate movement Tom Buchanan broke her nose with his open hand.

Then there were bloody towels on the bathroom floor, and angry women's voices, and high over the confusion a long broken cry of pain. Mr McKee woke from his sleep and started stiffly toward the door. Halfway there he turned around and stared at what was going on. His wife and Catherine were falling over the furniture as they moved about the crowded room, trying to help the bleeding figure on the sofa. Then Mr McKee turned and continued on out the door. I took up my hat and followed.

'Come to lunch some day,' he suggested, as we went down in the elevator.

'Where?'

'Anywhere.'

'All right,' I agreed. 'I'll be glad to.'

. . . I was standing beside his bed and he was sitting up between the sheets, wearing his underwear, with a great pile of photographs in his hands.

'Beauty and the Beast . . . Loneliness . . . Old Grocery Horse . . . Brooklyn Bridge . . .'

Then I was lying half asleep in the cold lower level of the Pennsylvania Station, staring at the morning newspaper, and waiting for the four o'clock train.

CHAPTER 3

A PARTY AT GATSBY'S

There was music from my neighbor's house through the summer nights. In his blue gardens, men and girls came and went like night-flying insects among the whisperings and the champagne and the stars. In the afternoons I watched his guests swimming from his private beach, and on weekends his Rolls-Royce became a bus, carrying people to and from the city between nine in the morning and long past midnight. And on Mondays eight servants, including an extra gardener, worked all day to make the house and garden perfect again after the weekend.

By seven o'clock every Saturday night, the orchestra has arrived. The last swimmers have come in from the beach and are dressing upstairs; there are at least five rows of cars from New York parked in front of the house, and already the halls and rooms are full of colorful dresses and the latest, strangest haircuts. Cocktails are being served in the garden, until the air is alive with cheerful talk and laughter, and introductions immediately forgotten, and enthusiastic meetings between women who never knew each other's names.

The lights grow brighter as the earth moves away from the sun, and now the orchestra is playing yellow cocktail music. The voices are louder and higher, and laughter is easier minute by minute. Suddenly a girl dances out alone on to the lawn, and the party has begun.

I believe that on the first night I went to Gatsby's house, I was one of the few guests who had actually been invited. People were not invited – they went there. They got into cars and ended up at Gatsby's door. Sometimes they arrived and departed without meeting their host at all.

But I had been actually invited. Early that Saturday morning Gatsby's driver, in a pale blue uniform, crossed my lawn with a surprisingly formal note from his employer, inviting me to his party that evening.

As soon as I arrived, I tried hard to find my host. But the two or three people I asked stared at me so strangely that I turned away from them and walked toward the safety of the cocktail table. It was the only place in the crowded garden where a single man could stand around without looking purposeless and alone.

After a while I saw Jordan Baker come out of the house and look down, with scornful interest, into the garden. I was delighted to see someone I recognized, and greeted her warmly.

'I thought you might be here,' she replied. 'I remembered you lived next door to—'

'Hello, Jordan!' cried two girls in yellow dresses, who were passing. 'Sorry you didn't win your match last week.'

They moved on, and with Jordan's slender golden arm resting in mine, we walked around the garden. Soon we sat down at a table with the two girls in yellow, and three men whose names I did not catch.

'Do you come to these parties often?' Jordan asked the girl beside her, whose name was Lucille.

'Yes, I like to come,' Lucille said. 'I never care what I do, so I always have a good time. When I was here last, I tore my dress on a chair, and he asked me my name and address. Well, in less than a week I got a parcel with a new evening dress in it.'

'Did you keep it?' asked Jordan.

'Sure I did. It cost two hundred and sixty-five dollars.'

'There's something about a man that'll do a thing like that,' said the other girl. 'He doesn't want any trouble with *any*body.'

'Who doesn't?' I asked.

'Gatsby. Somebody told me—' She lowered her voice. 'Somebody told me they thought he killed a man once.'

The three men bent forward and listened eagerly.

'I don't think it's so much *that*,' argued Lucille. 'It's more that he was a German spy during the war.'

One of the men agreed. 'I heard that from a man who grew up with him in Germany,' he said.

'Oh no,' said the other girl, 'it couldn't be that, because he was in the American army during the war.' She added enthusiastically, 'You look at him sometimes when he thinks nobody's looking at him. I'm sure he's killed a man.'

She narrowed her eyes and shivered. Lucille shivered. We all turned and looked for Gatsby, but there was no sign of him.

Supper was now being served, and Jordan invited me to eat with some of her friends at another table. But their conversation was polite and uninteresting, so she and I got up and told them we were going in search of our host.

The bar, where we looked first, was crowded, but Gatsby was not there. We tried an important-looking door, which opened into a beautiful library with a high ceiling.

A fat middle-aged man was sitting, rather drunk, on the edge of a great table, staring at the shelves of books all around him. His enormous glasses made him look owl-eyed. As we entered, he turned excitedly and spoke to us.

'What do you think?' he demanded.

'About what?' Jordan asked.

He waved his hand toward the books. 'About all these. You needn't bother to find out. *I* found out. They're real – they have pages and everything. I thought they'd have nothing inside, but – Here! Let me show you.' He rushed to a shelf and opened a book. 'See!' he cried delightedly. 'It's a real book! This Gatsby, what a library he's got!'

He put the book back on the shelf. 'I've been drunk for about a week now,' he added, 'and I thought it might help if I sat in a library for a while.'

'Has it helped?'

'I can't tell yet. I've only been here an hour. Did I tell you about the books? They're real. They're—'

'You told us.' We shook hands with him politely and went back outdoors.

There was dancing now on the lawn, the orchestra was playing jazz, and champagne was being served in glasses bigger than finger bowls. The moon had risen higher, and floating in the ocean was a silver triangle, trembling a little in the night air.

I was still with Jordan Baker, and I was enjoying myself now. We were sitting at a table with a man of about my age, and during a pause in the music he looked at me and smiled.

'I've seen you somewhere before,' he said politely. 'Weren't you in the army during the war?'

'Why, yes. I was in the First Infantry Division.'

'So was I, until June 1918. I knew I recognized you.'

We talked for a moment about some wet, gray little villages in France. Then he told me he had just bought a new motorboat and was going to try it out the next morning.

'Want to go with me, old sport?' he asked. 'Just off the beach near here. Any time that suits you best.'

'I'd like that,' I replied and added, 'This is an unusual party for me. I haven't even seen the host. I live next door, and this man Gatsby sent his driver over with an invitation.'

For a moment he didn't seem to know what I meant. Then he said suddenly, 'I'm Gatsby.'

'What!' I cried. 'Oh, I'm so sorry!'

'I thought you knew, old sport. I'm afraid I'm not a very good host.' He smiled understandingly. It was one of those smiles that you see only four or five times in your life. It

'This is an unusual party for me. I haven't even seen the host,' I said.

showed you that he understood you, believed in you, and had the best possible opinion of you. Suddenly it disappeared – and I was looking at a fashionably dressed young man, a year or two over thirty, who seemed to choose his words with great care.

The butler appeared, with the information that Chicago was calling Gatsby on the telephone.

'Excuse me,' he said, standing up. 'I have to go. If you want anything, just ask for it, old sport.'

When he was gone, I turned to Jordan impatiently. 'Who *is* he?' I demanded. 'Where is he from? And what does he do?'

'Now you're just like everyone else!' she replied smiling. 'He told me once he was an Oxford man. But I don't believe it.'

'Why not?'

'I don't know. I just don't think he went there.'

This made me even more curious than before. After a few minutes I caught sight of him. He had come out of the house and was standing there, looking in a pleased way at his guests. I could see nothing darkly mysterious about him at all. I wondered if the fact that he was not drinking made him appear different from the rest of us. It seemed to me that he grew more formal as everyone else behaved more wildly. There was no girl in his arms, or glass in his hand, or song on his lips.

'Excuse me, madam.' The butler was speaking to Jordan. 'Mr Gatsby would like to speak to you alone.'

'With me?' she said in surprise.

She got up slowly, and followed the butler toward the house.

An hour or so later she had not returned, and I decided to leave. As I was waiting for my hat in the hall, the library door opened, and Jordan and Gatsby came out together.

She came over to me and whispered, 'I've just heard the most surprising thing. Look, please come and see me. I'm staying at my aunt's . . . Mrs Sigourney Howard . . . phone book . . .' She was hurrying away as she spoke, to join her friends who were waiting to drive her home.

Feeling ashamed at staying so late, I went to say goodbye to Gatsby. I wanted to apologize for not knowing who he was.

'Don't give it another thought, old sport,' he said eagerly. 'And don't forget we're going out in the motorboat together tomorrow morning at nine o'clock.'

'Philadelphia wants you on the phone, sir,' said the butler behind his shoulder.

'Tell them I'll be right there,' he said. He smiled at me – and suddenly I was glad I was among the last to leave, because it seemed important to him. 'Good night, old sport . . . good night.'

Once I had reached my front door, I looked back across the lawn. A sudden emptiness seemed to flow now from the windows and the great doors of Gatsby's mansion. Standing on the porch was the lonely figure of the host, his hand raised in a formal goodbye.

That was a busy summer for me. I worked hard, learning the bond business. I began to like New York, especially the adventurous feel of it at night. I liked to walk up Fifth Avenue and choose romantic women from the crowd – I used to imagine that in a few minutes I was going to enter their lives, and no one would ever know. Sometimes I felt miserably lonely, and knew there were plenty of other young men who felt that way too.

For a while I lost sight of Jordan Baker, then in midsummer I found her again. At first I was delighted to go places with her, because everyone knew who she was. I wasn't actually in love, but I felt a strong interest in her. The bored, arrogant face she turned to the world was hiding something, and one day I found what it was. When we were at a house party together, she left a borrowed car out in the rain with the top down, and then lied about it. And suddenly the story came back to me, the one that I hadn't been able to remember that night at Daisy's. At her first big golf match someone had accused her of secretly moving her ball to a better position. In the end the story was covered up, but it made me realize that Jordan Baker was hopelessly dishonest. It made no difference to me – dishonesty in a woman is something you never blame deeply – and I soon forgot about it.

It was during that same house party that we had a strange conversation. It started because she drove so close to some workmen that her car touched a button on one man's coat.

'You're a rotten driver,' I protested. 'Either you ought to be more careful, or you oughtn't to drive at all.'

'I *am* careful.'

'No, you're not.'

'Well, other people are, and they'll keep out of my way.'

'Suppose you met someone just as careless as yourself?'

'I hope I never will,' she answered. 'I hate careless people. That's why I like you.'

For a moment I thought I loved her. But I said nothing. I knew that first I had to get myself out of that connection back home. For me, it had never been more than friendship, but there was a sort of understanding between us, and that had to be gently broken off before I was free.

Everyone believes they have at least one good point, and this is mine: I am one of the few honest people I have ever known.

CHAPTER 4

GATSBY'S PAST

At nine o'clock one morning in July, Gatsby's beautiful car arrived at my door. It was the first time he had called on me, although I had gone to two of his parties, been out in his motorboat and, at his urgent invitation, used his private beach.

'Good morning, old sport. You're having lunch with me today and I thought we'd drive up to town together.' He saw me looking admiringly at his car. 'It's pretty, isn't it, old sport? Haven't you seen it before?'

I'd seen it. Everybody had seen it. There was no other car like it in West Egg. Long and luxurious, it was a rich yellowish color. I got in and we started on the road to New York.

I had talked with him several times in the past month and found, to my disappointment, that he did not have much to say. So I was not expecting what happened next.

'Look here, old sport,' he said suddenly as we left West Egg village. 'What's your opinion of me?'

A little surprised, I gave the usual polite reply.

'I'm going to tell you something about my life,' he said. 'I don't want you to get the wrong idea from all these stories you hear. I'll tell you God's truth. I am the son of some wealthy people in the Middle West – all dead now. I was brought up in America, but educated at Oxford, like all my family before me.'

He looked at me sideways, and I knew why Jordan had believed he was lying. He swallowed the words 'educated at Oxford'. And with this doubt, I could not believe any of it.

'What part of the Middle West?' I asked innocently.

'San Francisco.'

'I see.'

'My family left me a good deal of money, so I lived like a king in all the capitals of Europe, collecting jewels, riding horses, painting a little, and trying to forget something very sad that had happened to me long ago.'

I managed not to laugh in his face. It was an old, old story, heard many times before – not even the words were new.

'Then came the war, old sport. I was glad to go and fight, and I tried very hard to die, but my life seemed to be protected in some magical way. I was sent to France as an army officer, and my men and I held an important position for two days and two nights against three German divisions. I was made a major, and received medals from all the countries on our side – even Montenegro, little Montenegro, down on the Adriatic Sea!'

I stared at him admiringly, wondering what he could possibly invent to tell me next. But he took a piece of metal from his pocket and put it in my hand.

'That's the medal from Montenegro.'

To my great surprise, the thing looked real. On the back was written, *To Major Jay Gatsby, for Extraordinary Bravery*.

'Here's another thing I always carry. A memory of Oxford days.' He showed me a photograph of six young men in the doorway of an ancient college; one of them was Gatsby.

So it was all true. I believed in him at last.

'I'm going to make a big request of you today,' he went on. 'That's why I thought you ought to know something about me. You'll hear about it this afternoon.'

'At lunch?'

'No, this afternoon. I happened to find out that you're taking Miss Baker to tea. She has kindly agreed to speak to you about this matter.'

I had no idea what 'this matter' was, but I was more annoyed than interested. I hadn't asked Jordan Baker to tea in order to discuss Mr Jay Gatsby.

As we drove at high speed into New York, we were stopped by a policeman on a motorbike.

'All right, old sport,' called Gatsby. He took a white card from his pocket and waved it at the policeman.

'Right you are,' agreed the policeman politely. 'I'll know you next time, Mr Gatsby. Excuse *me*!'

'What was that?' I asked Gatsby. 'The picture of Oxford?'

'I was able to help the chief of police once, and he sends me a card every year.'

We drove over the great bridge, with the sunlight on the moving cars, and the city rising up across the river. New York seen from the Queensboro Bridge is always the city seen for the first time, in its first wild promise of all the mystery and the beauty in the world.

'Anything can happen now that we've come over this bridge,' I thought, 'anything at all . . .'

Even Gatsby could happen, without any particular wonder.

• —— •

By midday it was very hot. I left my office and met Gatsby for lunch, in a cool Forty-second Street restaurant. When I arrived, he was there already, talking to another man.

'Mr Carraway, this is my friend Mr Wolfshiem,' Gatsby said to me.

Wolfshiem was a small, flat-nosed man of about fifty, with a large head and two tiny eyes.

'So I took one look at him,' said Mr Wolfshiem, shaking my hand, 'and what do you think I did?'

'What?' I asked politely.

It turned out, however, that he was not speaking to me, but to Gatsby.

'I handed the money to Katspaugh and I said, "All right, Katspaugh, don't pay him a cent until he shuts his mouth." He shut it then and there.' Mr Wolfshiem gave a pleased smile.

Gatsby took both of us by the arm and moved us toward a table. The head waiter brought cocktails.

Mr Wolfshiem turned to me. 'I understand you're looking for a business connection,' he said.

Gatsby said quickly, 'Oh no, this isn't the man.'

'No?' Mr Wolfshiem seemed disappointed.

'This is just a friend. I told you we'd talk about that some other time.'

The food arrived, and we started eating.

'Look here, old sport,' said Gatsby, turning to me. 'I'm afraid I made you a little angry this morning in the car.' There was the smile again, but this time I was able to fight against it.

'I don't like mysteries,' I said, 'and I don't understand why you won't tell me honestly what you want. Why has it all got to come through Miss Baker?'

'Oh, it's nothing unpleasant, I promise you. Miss Baker's a great sportswoman, you know, and she'd never do anything that wasn't all right.'

Suddenly he looked at his watch, jumped up and left the room, leaving me and Mr Wolfshiem together.

'He has to telephone,' said Mr Wolfshiem. 'Fine man, isn't he? Handsome to look at, and perfect manners. He went to one of the most famous colleges in the world – Oxford College in England. You know it?'

'I've heard of it,' I said. 'Have you known him long?'

'Since just after the war. It only took me an hour to discover he was a man of good family and education. I said to myself, "There's the kind of man you'd like to take home and introduce to your mother and sister."' He paused. 'I see you're looking at my shirt buttons.'

I hadn't been looking at them, but I did now.

'Finest examples of human teeth,' he informed me.

'Well!' I said. 'That's a very interesting idea.'

'Yes.' He went on, 'Gatsby's very careful about women. He would never even look at a friend's wife.'

Soon after Gatsby's return, Mr Wolfshiem finished his coffee, said goodbye and left us.

'Who is he?' I asked Gatsby. 'An actor? A dentist?'

'Meyer Wolfshiem? No, he's a gambler. You remember the 1919 World Series? Wolfshiem's the man who paid eight of the Chicago players to let the other team win. He made a lot of money out of it.'

'Why isn't he in prison?'

'They can't get him, old sport. He's a smart man.'

At that moment I saw Tom Buchanan across the crowded room. He came over to our table and I introduced him to Gatsby. They shook hands, and to my surprise Gatsby looked quite uncomfortable. Tom and I said a few words to each other, and when I turned back to Gatsby, he was no longer there.

•——•

One October day in nineteen-seventeen . . .
(said Jordan Baker that afternoon, sitting up very straight in the tea-garden at the Plaza Hotel)
. . . I was walking past Daisy Fay's house.

Daisy was just eighteen then, two years older than me, and by far the most popular girl in Louisville – all day long the telephone rang in her house and excited young officers asked to take her out.

When I came opposite her house that morning, I saw her sitting in her little white car with an officer I'd never seen before. He was looking at her in such a romantic way that I've never forgotten it. His name was Jay Gatsby, and I didn't see him again for over four years.

Then one night that winter her mother found her packing a bag to go to New York and say goodbye to an officer who was going overseas. Her family stopped her going, but she didn't speak to them for weeks. A year and a half later, she married Tom Buchanan. He hired a whole floor of Louisville's best hotel for his guests, and the day before the wedding he gave her a necklace which cost three hundred and fifty thousand dollars.

I was her best friend by then, and the night before the wedding I went into her room just before dinner. I found her lying on her bed as lovely as the June night in her flowered dress – and as drunk as a monkey. She had a bottle of wine in one hand and a letter in the other.

'Congratulate me,' she called out. 'Never had a drink before, but oh, how I do enjoy it!'

'What's the matter, Daisy?' I was scared, I can tell you; I'd never seen a girl like that before.

'Here, my dear.' She felt drunkenly around on the floor, and picked up the necklace. 'Give it back to whoever it belongs to. And tell them all, Daisy's changed her mind!'

She began to cry – she cried and cried. I rushed out and found her mother's servant girl. We locked the door and got Daisy into a cold bath. She wouldn't let go of the letter and kept it in the bath with her, until it came to pieces like snow. But she didn't say another word. We put ice on her forehead and buttoned her up in her dress, and half an hour later, when we walked out of the room, the necklace was round her neck and it was all over. Next day at five o'clock she married Tom Buchanan without so much as a shiver.

I saw them later that summer in Santa Barbara, and I thought I'd never seen a girl so mad about her husband. It was touching to see her with Tom. That was in August. One night a week later, Tom had a car accident, and there was a photograph of him in the local newspaper. The girl who was with him got into the papers too – she was a waitress at the Santa Barbara Hotel.

The next April Daisy had her little girl, and they went to France for a year. They came back to Chicago, and then moved to Long Island. About six weeks ago, she heard the name Gatsby for the first time in years, when I asked you – do you remember? – if you knew Gatsby in West Egg. After you had gone home, she came to my room and asked me, 'What Gatsby?' And when I described him, she said in the strangest voice that it must be the man she used to know. It wasn't until then that I connected this Gatsby with the officer sitting in her little white car.

• —— •

By the time Jordan had finished, we were in a horse-drawn cab, driving through Central Park in the warm half-light.

'It was a strange coincidence,' I said.

'But it wasn't a coincidence at all. Gatsby bought that house so that Daisy would be just across the bay.'

So when I saw him on his lawn that June night, stretching out his arms, it wasn't just the stars that he wanted to touch. He came alive to me; suddenly his shallow life of great wealth and parties had a deeper purpose.

'He half expected her to come to one of his parties, but she never did,' continued Jordan. 'Now he wants to know if you'll

Daisy came to my room and asked me, 'What Gatsby?'

invite her to your house one afternoon and let him come over.'

It was so little to ask. He had waited five years and bought a mansion – so that he could 'come over' to a stranger's garden.

'Why didn't he ask you to arrange a meeting?'

'He wants her to see his house, and you live right next door.'

It was dark now, and I put my arm round Jordan's golden shoulder and drew her toward me. Suddenly I wasn't thinking of Daisy and Gatsby any more, but of this clean, hard, limited person, who believed in nothing and who sat confidently within the circle of my arm.

'And Daisy ought to have something in her life,' she added.

'Does she want to see Gatsby?'

'He doesn't want her to know about this. You're just supposed to invite her to tea.'

We passed a line of dark trees, and then the lights of Fifty-ninth Street shone down into the park. Unlike Gatsby and Tom Buchanan, I had no girl to dream about, so I drew up the girl beside me, tightening my arms. Her pale, scornful mouth smiled, and so I drew her up again closer, this time to my face.

CHAPTER 5

GATSBY AND DAISY MEET AGAIN

When I came home to West Egg that night, I was afraid for a moment that my house was on fire. Two o'clock in the morning, and the whole of the coastline seemed to be in flames. Turning a corner, I saw that it was Gatsby's house, lit from tower to cellar.

At first I thought it was another party. But there wasn't a sound, only wind in the trees. As my taxi drove away, I saw Gatsby walking toward me across his lawn.

'Every light in your house must be on,' I said.

He turned his eyes toward it absently. 'I've been looking into some of the rooms. Let's go for a drive, old sport.'

'It's too late.'

'All right.' He waited, trying to hide his eagerness.

'I talked with Miss Baker,' I said after a moment. 'I'm going to call up Daisy tomorrow and invite her over here to tea.'

'Oh, I don't want to put you to any trouble,' he said.

'What day would suit you?' I asked.

'What day would suit *you*?' he corrected me quickly.

'How about the day after tomorrow?'

He hesitated. 'I want to get the grass cut,' he said. I suspected that he meant my untidy lawn. 'There's another thing,' he added uncertainly. 'You don't make much money, old sport, do you?'

'Not very much.'

He went on more confidently, 'You see, I carry on a little business. I think it would interest you. It wouldn't take up much of your time and you might pick up a nice bit of money.'

He was obviously making this offer because I was going to help him meet Daisy, so I didn't feel I could accept. I refused politely. After another attempt at conversation, he went home.

I called up Daisy from the office next morning and invited her to come to tea. 'Don't bring Tom,' I warned her.

'Who is "Tom"?' she asked innocently.

The following day it was pouring with rain. At eleven o'clock Gatsby's gardener came over to cut my wet grass, and I drove into West Egg village to search for my Finnish woman and to buy some cakes and cups and flowers. The flowers were unnecessary, because at two o'clock a car arrived from Gatsby's, delivering a mountain of roses, with vases to put them in.

An hour later the front door opened nervously, and Gatsby hurried in. He was pale, and there were dark signs of sleeplessness under his eyes.

'Is everything all right?' he asked immediately.

'The grass looks fine, if that's what you mean.'

'What grass?' he asked vacantly. 'Oh yes, your grass.' He looked out at it, but I don't believe he saw a thing.

'Have you got everything you need for – for tea?'

I showed him the twelve little cakes from the baker's.

'Will they do?' I asked.

'Of course, of course! They're fine!' and he added hollowly, 'old sport.'

By half-past three the rain had slowed to a heavy wet mist. Gatsby sat there, looking with unseeing eyes through my magazines. Finally he stood up and told me he was going home.

'Why's that?'

'Nobody's coming to tea. It's too late!' He looked nervously at his watch. 'I can't wait all day.'

'Don't be silly. It's just two minutes to four.'

He sat down miserably, and at that moment we heard a car arriving. We both jumped up, and I went outside.

From the car window Daisy's face looked out at me, from under a three-cornered hat, with a delighted smile.

'Is this absolutely where you live, my dearest one?'

Her lovely voice made the gray day feel brighter. I took her hand to help her from the car.

'Are you in love with me?' she said low in my ear. 'If not, why did I have to come alone?'

'That's my secret. Tell your driver to go away for an hour.'

We went indoors. To my surprise, the living room was deserted. There was a light knocking at the front door. When I opened it, Gatsby was standing on the doorstep, pale as death, with his hands deep in his coat pockets. Without a word, he walked past me into the living room.

For half a minute there wasn't a sound. Then I heard a sort of murmur and part of a laugh, followed by Daisy's voice on a clear, false note: 'I certainly am awfully glad to see you again.'

There was a pause. It lasted a horribly long time. I had nothing to do in the hall, so I went into the living room.

Gatsby, his hands still in his pockets, was standing in front of the fireplace. The back of his head was touching a clock on a shelf, but he was trying to look perfectly comfortable and even a little bored. His miserable eyes stared down at Daisy, who was sitting, frightened but beautiful, on the edge of a stiff chair.

'We've met before,' murmured Gatsby. Luckily the clock chose this moment to fall off the shelf, so he turned and caught it with trembling fingers. 'I'm sorry about the clock,' he said.

I couldn't think of a single sensible thing to say. 'It's an old clock,' I told them stupidly. I think we all believed for a moment that it had smashed in pieces on the floor.

'We haven't met for many years,' said Daisy, almost calmly.

'Five years next November.'

The automatic quality of Gatsby's answer made us all feel even more embarrassed. I made the desperate suggestion that they help me make tea in the kitchen, and they were both on their feet when the Finnish woman brought the teapot in.

In the welcome confusion of cups and cakes, things were better. Gatsby sat down in the shadows, and watched Daisy and me talking, with dark, unhappy eyes. But at the first possible moment I got up and said I had to leave them.

'Where are you going?' demanded Gatsby in immediate alarm. 'I've got to speak to you before you go.' He followed me wildly into the kitchen, closed the door, and whispered, 'Oh, God!' in a miserable way.

'What's the matter?'

'This is a terrible mistake, a terrible, terrible mistake.'

'You're just embarrassed, that's all,' and luckily I added, 'Daisy's embarrassed too.'

This came as a great surprise to him.

'You're behaving like a little boy,' I went on. 'Not only that, 'but you're being rude. Daisy's sitting in there all alone.'

Frowning, he raised his hand to stop my words, and, opening the door cautiously, went back into the living room.

I walked out the back way – just as Gatsby had done half an hour earlier – and waited under a huge black tree in the middle of my lawn. Once more it was pouring, and there was nothing to look at from under the tree except Gatsby's enormous mansion.

After half an hour the sun shone again. The rain had

sounded like the murmur of their voices, but in the new silence, I felt that silence had fallen within the house too.

I went in – after making every possible noise in the kitchen – but I don't believe they heard a sound. They were sitting at either end of the sofa, and every sign of embarrassment was gone. Daisy had been crying, and was drying her tears. But there was a surprising change in Gatsby. He simply shone with delight; his new-found happiness filled the little room.

'Oh, hello, old sport,' he said. I could have been a friend he hadn't seen for years. I thought for a moment he was going to shake hands.

'It's stopped raining.'

'Has it?' When he realized what I was talking about, he smiled and repeated the news to Daisy. 'What do you think of that? It's stopped raining.'

'I'm glad, Jay.' Her throat, full of achingly sad beauty, told only of her unexpected joy.

'I want you and Daisy to come over to my house,' he said. 'I'd like to show her around.'

'You're sure you want me to come?'

'Absolutely, old sport.'

Daisy went upstairs to wash her face, while Gatsby and I waited on the lawn.

'My house looks well, doesn't it?' he demanded.

I agreed that it was very handsome.

'Yes.' His eyes went over every detail of it. 'It took me just three years to earn the money that bought it.'

'I thought you inherited your money.'

'I did, old sport,' he said automatically, 'but I lost most of it when the money markets crashed after the war.'

Before I could answer, Daisy came out of the house.

'That huge place *there*?' she cried, pointing.

'Do you like it?'

'I love it, but I don't see how you live there all alone.'

'I keep it always full of interesting people, night and day. People who do interesting things. Famous people.'

Instead of taking the short cut across the lawn, we walked down to the road and entered through the main gates. With murmurs of delight Daisy admired the flowers, the gardens, and the way the mansion stood out against the sky.

Inside, as we wandered through music rooms and sitting rooms, I felt there were guests hidden behind every sofa and table, under orders to be breathlessly silent until we had passed by. As Gatsby closed the door of the library, I was almost sure I heard the owl-eyed man break into ghostly laughter.

Upstairs, we saw luxuriously furnished bedrooms with fresh flowers on the tables, dressing rooms, and bathrooms. Finally we came to Gatsby's own apartment, where we sat down and drank a glass of wine from a bottle he kept in a cupboard.

He hadn't once stopped looking at Daisy. Sometimes too, he stared around in a dazed way at the valuable things he owned, thinking perhaps that in her actual presence they weren't real any longer. After his embarrassment and then his unreasoning joy, he now felt only wonder that she was there.

Pulling himself together, he opened two huge cupboards to show us his well-cut suits, expensive shirts, and silk ties.

'I've got a man in England who buys me clothes. He sends over some things for me to choose from, twice a year.'

He took out a pile of shirts and threw them down in front of us. They covered the table in many-colored confusion. While we admired, the soft rich heap grew higher. Suddenly Daisy bent her head into the shirts and began to cry stormily.

'They're such beautiful shirts,' she sobbed. 'It makes me sad because I've never seen such – such beautiful shirts before.'

Outside Gatsby's window it began to rain again, and we stood in a row looking out at the sea beyond the lawn.

'If it wasn't so misty, we could see your home across the bay,' said Gatsby. 'You always have a green light that burns all night at the end of your dock.'

Daisy put her arm through his, but Gatsby seemed lost in thought. Possibly he had realized that the enormous importance of that light had now gone for ever. To him it had seemed very near to her, almost touching her, as close as a star to the moon. Now it was just a green light on a dock again.

'Look!' cried Daisy. The darkness had parted in the west, and there were pink and golden clouds above the sea.

She whispered, 'I'd like to just get one of those pink clouds and put you in it and push you around.'

I tried to go then, but they wouldn't hear of it. Perhaps my presence made them feel more satisfactorily alone.

'I know what we'll do,' said Gatsby, 'we'll have Klipspringer play the piano for us.' Klipspringer was a young man who lived at Gatsby's most of the time – he did not seem to have any other home.

Gatsby went to find Klipspringer, and we all went downstairs to the music room.

Gatsby lit Daisy's cigarette with a trembling hand and sat down with her on a sofa far across the room, in the shadows, while Klipspringer started playing.

When he had finished the first piece, Klipspringer turned around and searched unhappily for Gatsby in the darkness.

'I'm all out of practice, you see. I told you I couldn't play.'

'Don't talk so much, old sport,' commanded Gatsby. 'Play!'

'I'd like to just get one of those pink clouds and put you in it and push you around,' whispered Daisy.

In the morning,
In the evening,
Ain't we got fun—

Outside the wind was loud. All the lights were going on in West Egg now; the electric trains were carrying men home from New York, and there was excitement in the air.

One thing's sure and nothing's surer,
The rich get rich and the poor get – children.
In the meantime,
In between time—

As I went over to say goodbye, I saw the dazed look on Gatsby's face again. Was he doubting the quality of his happiness? Almost five years! There must have been moments, even that afternoon, when Daisy disappointed him a little – not through her own fault, but because of the enormous vitality of his dream. It had gone beyond her, beyond everything. He had thrown his whole being into creating it, adding to it every bright feather that came his way. No fire or freshness can challenge what a man can keep safe in his ghostly heart.

While I watched him, his hand took hold of hers, and as she said something low in his ear, he turned toward her with a sudden rush of feeling. I think that feverish, exciting voice of hers held him most, because it couldn't be dreamed – that voice was a deathless song.

They had forgotten me, but Daisy looked up and held out her hand; Gatsby didn't know me now at all. I looked once more at them and they looked back at me, distantly, enclosed in their own bright world. Then I went out of the room and down the grand steps into the rain, leaving them there together.

CHAPTER 6

THE TRUTH ABOUT GATSBY

That summer there were many wild stories about Gatsby, as the hundreds of people who attended his parties told their friends about him, using their imagination to fill in details of his present and past. Exactly why these wild stories were so pleasing to James Gatz of North Dakota isn't easy to say.

James Gatz – that was his real name. He had changed it at the age of seventeen and at the exact moment that saw the start of his new life – when he saw Dan Cody's yacht drop anchor in one of the most dangerous parts of Lake Superior. He was James Gatz as he walked aimlessly along the beach that afternoon in a torn green jacket and a pair of old trousers, but when he borrowed a boat, rowed out to the yacht, and informed Cody that a wind might catch it and break it up in half an hour, he had already become Jay Gatsby.

I suppose he'd had the name ready for a long time, even then. His parents were lazy, unsuccessful farm people, and in his head he never thought of them as his parents at all. He invented just the sort of Jay Gatsby that a seventeen-year-old would be likely to invent, and he went on believing in this invention to the end.

For over a year he had been making his way along the south shore of Lake Superior, fishing or doing any other work that paid for his food and bed. His brown, hardening body lived naturally through the half-fierce, half-lazy work of the cold windy days. He knew women early, and because they offered themselves willingly to him, he became scornful of them.

But his heart was never at peace. The wildest, most fantastic dreams kept him awake at night, while the moonlight shone in on the untidy heap of his clothes on the floor. He was sure that a great future lay ahead of him. He was still searching for it, on the day that Dan Cody's yacht dropped anchor in the lake.

Cody was fifty years old then, and extremely wealthy, as he had made several fortunes in the Nevada silver fields and the Yukon gold rush. A large number of women had tried to separate him from his money, and some had succeeded, especially the latest, Ella Kaye. At the moment, however, he was sailing alone.

To young Gatz, looking up from his rowing boat, that yacht represented all the beauty and power in the world. I suppose he smiled at Cody – he had probably discovered that people liked him when he smiled. Anyway, Cody asked him a few questions and found that he was quick and extremely ambitious. A few days later, Cody bought him some yachting clothes, and when the yacht left for the West Indies, Gatsby left too.

He was paid to cook the meals, serve the drinks, sail the yacht, and write Cody's letters. Sometimes he was even told to lock up his employer; Cody was a hard drinker, who knew he was likely to do stupid things when he was drunk. The arrangement lasted for five years. It would probably have lasted for longer, except for the fact that Ella Kaye arrived on the yacht one night in Boston, and a week later Dan Cody died.

It was from Cody that Gatsby inherited money – Cody left him twenty-five thousand dollars at his death. But Gatsby didn't get it. The law was used against him in some way, and he never understood how it was done. What remained of Cody's millions went untouched to Ella Kaye. Gatsby was left with an unusually valuable education; the shadowy figure of Jay Gatsby had filled out to become a solid, real person.

He told me all this much later, but I've put it down here, with the idea of exploding those first wild stories about his past, which weren't even partly true.

For several weeks after I had invited Daisy to tea, I didn't see Gatsby. Mostly I was in New York, going out with Jordan and trying to endear myself to her ancient aunt. Finally I went over to his house one Sunday afternoon. I hadn't been there two minutes when somebody brought Tom Buchanan in for a drink. There were three of them – Tom, a man named Sloane, and a pretty woman who had been there before.

'I'm delighted to see you,' said Gatsby. 'Sit right down. Have a cigarette.' He walked round the room quickly, ringing bells. 'I'll have something to drink for you in just a minute.'

He was uneasy because Tom was there. But he also felt uncomfortable until he had given them something, realizing that that was all they came for. There was a little polite conversation; then Gatsby, unable to stop himself, spoke suddenly to Tom.

'I believe we've met somewhere before, Mr Buchanan.'

'Oh, yes,' said Tom, obviously not remembering. 'So we did. I remember very well.'

'I know your wife,' continued Gatsby, in a challenging way.

'Is that so?' Tom turned to me. 'You live near here, Nick?'

'Next door.'

Mr Sloane said nothing, and nor did the woman. But after two cocktails she became more friendly.

'We'll all come over to your next party, Mr Gatsby,' she suggested. 'What do you say?'

'Certainly. I'd be delighted to have you.'

'We ought to start for home,' said Mr Sloane, unsmiling.

'Please don't hurry,' said Gatsby. He had control of himself now, and he wanted to see more of Tom. 'Why don't you – why don't you stay for supper?'

'You come to supper with *me*,' said the lady enthusiastically. 'Both of you.' This included me. Mr Sloane got to his feet.

'Come along,' he said, but to her only.

Gatsby looked at me questioningly. He wanted to go but he didn't see that Mr Sloane was determined he shouldn't.

'I'm afraid I won't be able to,' I said.

'I'll follow you in my car,' said Gatsby. 'I'll get my coat.'

The rest of us walked out on the porch, where Sloane and the lady began an angry conversation.

'My God, I believe the man's coming,' Tom said to me. 'Doesn't he realize she doesn't want him? She's arranged a big dinner party and he won't know anyone there.' He frowned. 'I wonder where he met Daisy. By God, my ideas may be a little out of date, but I think women run around too much these days. They meet all kinds of crazy fish.'

Suddenly Mr Sloane and the lady walked down the steps.

'Come on,' said Mr Sloane over his shoulder to Tom, 'we're late.' And then to me, 'Tell him we couldn't wait, will you?'

Tom and I shook hands, and the three of them departed, just as Gatsby, with hat and light overcoat in hand, came out of the front door.

Tom was obviously concerned about Daisy's running around alone, because on the following Saturday night he came with her to Gatsby's party. Perhaps his presence gave the evening its peculiarly threatening quality – it stands out in my memory from Gatsby's other parties that summer. There were the same people, or at least the same sort of people, the same generous provision of champagne, the same colorful confusion, but I felt an unpleasantness in the air that hadn't been there before. Or perhaps it was just that I had grown used to it, grown to accept West Egg as a world complete in itself, and now I was looking at it again, through Daisy's eyes.

They arrived as darkness was beginning to fall, and Daisy's lovely voice was playing murmuring tricks in her throat, as we walked out among the hundreds of guests on the lawn.

'These things excite me *so*,' she whispered. 'If you want to kiss me at any time during the evening, Nick, just let me know and I'll be glad to arrange it for you. Just mention my name. Or present a green card. I'm giving out green—'

'Look around,' suggested Gatsby. 'You must see the faces of many people you've heard about.'

Tom's arrogant eyes searched the crowd. 'I was just thinking, I don't know anyone here.'

Gatsby took Tom and Daisy from group to group, introducing them to actors, film directors, singers, sportsmen, businessmen.

'I've never met so many famous people!' cried Daisy.

She and Gatsby danced. I was surprised by his beautiful dancing – I'd never seen him dance before. Then they walked over to my house and sat on the steps for half an hour, while at Daisy's request I remained watchfully in the garden. 'In case there's a fire or a flood,' she explained, 'or any act of God.'

Tom reappeared as we were sitting down to supper together.

'Do you mind if I eat with some people over there?' he asked. 'A man's started telling some jokes.'

'Go ahead,' answered Daisy cheerfully, 'and if you want to take down any addresses, here's my little gold pencil.' She looked around after a moment and told me that the girl was 'coarse but pretty'. I knew that except for the half hour she'd been alone with Gatsby, she wasn't having a good time.

Daisy and Gatsby danced.

Later on, I sat on the front steps with Tom and Daisy, while they waited for their driver to bring the car to the door.

'Who is this Gatsby, anyway?' demanded Tom suddenly. 'Some big bootlegger?'

'Where did you hear that?' I asked.

'I didn't hear it. I imagined it. A lot of these newly rich people are just big bootleggers, you know.'

'Not Gatsby,' I said shortly.

He was silent for a moment. 'Well, he certainly must have worked hard to get this crowd of crazy people together.'

'At least they're more interesting than the people we know,' Daisy said.

'You didn't look so interested.'

'Well, I was.'

'I'd like to know what he is and what he does,' insisted Tom. 'And I think I'll make a point of finding out.'

'I can tell you right now,' she answered. 'He owned some drug-stores, a lot of them. He built up the business himself.'

Their car arrived and they got in.

'Good night, Nick,' said Daisy.

She looked away from me and up to the top of the steps. We could hear *Three o'clock in the Morning*, a neat, sad little dance song, coming from the open door. What was it in the song that seemed to be calling her back inside? What would happen now in the soft hours of darkness? Perhaps some unbelievable guest would arrive, some lovely, bright-eyed young girl who with one look at Gatsby, in one magic, romantic moment, would undo those five years of unchanging love.

I stayed late that night, because Gatsby asked me to wait until he was free. When he came down the steps to the garden, where I was waiting, his eyes were tired.

'She didn't like it,' he said immediately.

'Of course she did.'

'She didn't like it,' he insisted. 'She didn't have a good time.'

He was silent, and I guessed at his deep sadness.

'I feel far away from her,' he said. 'It's hard to make her understand.'

'You mean about the dance?'

'The dance?' He waved the idea away scornfully. 'Old sport, the dance is unimportant.'

He wanted nothing less of Daisy than that she should go to Tom and say, 'I never loved you.' Then she and Gatsby could decide what to do next. After she was free, he wanted them to return to Louisville and be married from her house – just as he had intended five years ago.

'And she doesn't understand,' he said. 'She used to be able to understand. We'd sit for hours—'

'I wouldn't ask too much of her,' I said daringly. 'You can't repeat the past.'

'Can't repeat the past!' he cried, shocked. 'Why, of course you can!' He looked around him wildly. He seemed to think the past was hiding here in the shadow of his house, just out of reach of his hand.

'I'm going to fix everything just the way it was before,' he said determinedly. 'She'll see.'

He talked a lot about the past, and I understood that he wanted to rediscover something, some idea of himself perhaps, that had gone into loving Daisy. His life had been confused and meaningless since then, but if he could only return to a certain starting place and go over it all slowly, he could find out what that thing was . . .

. . . One autumn night, five years before, they had been

walking down the street. The ground was white with moonlight, and they stopped and turned toward each other. It was a cool night, but with that mysterious excitement in it which comes as the seasons change. Out of the corner of his eye, Gatsby saw that the houses on the street made a kind of ladder, which reached up to a secret place above the trees. He could climb to it, if he climbed alone, and once he was there he could drink the milk of life.

His heart beat faster and faster as Daisy's white face came up to his own. He knew that when he kissed this girl, he would never dream his wild dreams again. So he waited, listening for a moment longer to the music of the stars. Then he kissed her. At the touch of his lips, love opened like a flower and his new life was born.

Through all he said – and it was horribly over-romantic – I was reminded of something I had heard somewhere a long time ago. Words tried to take shape in my mouth, and my lips parted like a dumb man's. But they made no sound, and what I had almost remembered was forgotten for ever.

CHAPTER 7

A HOT DAY IN TOWN

One Saturday night the lights in Gatsby's house failed to go on, and as confusingly as it had begun, his life as a party-giver was over. Cars came eagerly up to his house, stayed just for a minute, then drove crossly away. Wondering if he were sick, I went over to find out, but I was turned away by a butler I did not recognize, who was rude and unhelpful. My Finnish woman informed me that Gatsby had sent away all his servants a week ago, replacing them with new ones, who never went into West Egg village.

Next day Gatsby called me on the phone.

'Going away?' I asked.

'No, old sport.'

'I hear you've got new servants.'

'I wanted people who wouldn't talk about me in the village. Daisy comes over quite often – in the afternoons.'

So the parties and the famous people, the music and the dancing – he had thrown this kind of life away because Daisy didn't like it.

'Look, old sport, Daisy asked me to ring you. Will you come to lunch at her house tomorrow? Miss Baker will be there.'

I accepted, wondering what was going to happen. I couldn't believe Daisy and Gatsby would choose this occasion to tell Tom about their affair.

The next day was almost the last, certainly the warmest, of the summer. At the Buchanans' house we were shown into the sitting room, which was cool and shaded from the sun. Daisy and Jordan lay on an enormous sofa in their white dresses.

'It's so hot, we can't move,' they said together.

We could hear Tom's voice, speaking on the hall phone. Gatsby stood in the center of the red carpet and looked around with great interest. Daisy watched him and laughed her sweet, exciting laugh.

'We think,' whispered Jordan, 'that that's Tom's girl on the telephone.'

The voice in the hall rose high with annoyance.

'Very well, then, I won't sell you the car at all. And don't bother me at lunch-time again, do you understand?'

'He's got his hand over the phone,' said Daisy bitterly.

'No, he hasn't,' I said. 'He's doing business with this man. I happen to know about it.'

Tom came in. Hiding his dislike, he greeted Gatsby, and after shaking hands with me, went out again to get some drinks. As he left the room, Daisy got up and went over to Gatsby. She pulled his face down and kissed him on the mouth.

'You know I love you,' she murmured.

'You forget there's a lady present,' said Jordan.

Daisy looked round doubtfully. 'You kiss Nick too.'

'What a low, coarse girl you are!'

'I don't care!' cried Daisy, and danced a few steps. Then, remembering the heat, she sat down guiltily, just as a nurse came into the room with a little girl.

'My dearest love!' Daisy almost sang, while holding out her arms. 'Come to your own mother who loves you!'

The child rushed across the room into Daisy's arms. Gatsby was looking at the little girl in surprise; I don't think he had ever really believed she existed.

'How do you like Mother's friends?' Daisy turned her around to look straight at Gatsby. 'Do you think they're pretty?'

'Where's Daddy?'

'She doesn't look like her father,' Daisy explained to us. 'She looks like me. Goodbye, my dearest one!'

The nurse took the child's hand and they left the room, just as Tom came back, carrying four large cocktails.

We drank in long, greedy swallows. There was a little conversation, but the heat was making us all tired. Lunch was in the dining room, which was also darkened against the heat.

'What'll we do with ourselves this afternoon?' cried Daisy, 'And the day after that, and the next thirty years?'

'Don't be sad,' Jordan said. 'Life starts all over again when it gets cold in the autumn.'

'But it's so hot,' insisted Daisy, on the edge of tears, 'and everything's so confused. Let's all go to town!'

Gatsby's eyes turned toward her.

'Ah,' she cried, 'you look so cool!'

Their eyes met, and they stared at each other. No one else existed for them in that moment – they were alone.

'You always look so cool,' she repeated.

She had told him she loved him, and Tom Buchanan saw. He couldn't believe it. His mouth dropped open, and he looked at Gatsby and then back at Daisy.

'All right,' he said. 'I'm perfectly willing to go to town.' He got up, his eyes still on his wife and Gatsby. No one moved.

'Come on!' he said angrily. 'If we're going, let's start.'

'Are we just going to go like this?' said Daisy. 'Aren't we going to let anyone smoke a cigarette first?'

'Everybody smoked all through lunch.'

'Let's have fun,' she begged him. 'It's too hot to get cross.'

He didn't answer.

'Have it your own way,' she said. 'Come on, Jordan.'

They went upstairs to get ready while we three men waited silently outside the front door.

'I don't see the point of going to town,' said Tom suddenly and fiercely. 'Women get these silly ideas in their heads—'

'Shall we take anything to drink?' called Daisy from an upstairs window.

'I'll get some whisky,' said Tom, and went inside.

Gatsby turned to me. 'I can't say anything in his house.'

'Her voice gives away more than she realizes,' I said. 'It's full of . . .' I hesitated.

'Her voice is full of money,' he said suddenly.

That was it. I'd never understood before. That was the endless magic that rose and fell in it, the music of it . . . High in a white palace the king's daughter, the golden girl . . .

Tom came out of the house wrapping a large bottle of whisky in a towel. Daisy and Jordan came out too, wearing small tight hats.

'Shall we all go in my car?' suggested Gatsby.

'No,' said Tom, 'you take my coupé and let me drive yours.'

The suggestion was distasteful to Gatsby. 'I don't think there's much gas,' he protested.

'If necessary, I can stop at a drug-store,' said Tom. He added unpleasantly, 'You can buy anything there these days.'

A pause followed this remark. Daisy frowned at Tom, and a strange expression passed over Gatsby's face.

'Come on, Daisy,' said Tom, pressing her with his hand toward Gatsby's car. 'I'll take you in this crazy machine.'

He opened the door, but she moved out from the circle of his arm.

'You take Nick and Jordan. We'll follow in your car.'

She walked close to Gatsby, touching his coat with her hand.

Jordan, Tom and I got into Gatsby's car and Tom drove away fast, into the heavy heat.

'Did you see that?' demanded Tom.

'See what?'

He looked at us closely, realizing that Jordan and I must have known, all the time. 'You think I'm pretty dumb, don't you?' He paused, and went on, 'Well, I've been investigating this man and his past.'

'And you found he was an Oxford man,' said Jordan helpfully.

'An Oxford man!' he laughed. 'He wears a pink suit!'

'Listen, Tom, if you think he's no good, why did you invite him to lunch?' demanded Jordan crossly.

'Daisy invited him. She knew him before we were married – God knows where!'

After that, we drove for a while in silence. Then as Doctor T. J. Eckleburg's pale eyes came into sight, I remembered Gatsby's warning about the gasoline.

'We've got enough to get us into town,' said Tom sharply.

'But there's a garage right here,' said Jordan.

Tom braked impatiently, and we stopped under Wilson's dusty sign. After a moment the garage owner came out and stared, hollow-eyed, at the car.

'Let's have some gas!' cried Tom roughly. 'What do you think we stopped for – to admire the view?'

'I'm sick,' said Wilson without moving. 'Been sick all day.'

'Well, shall I help myself?' Tom demanded. 'You sounded well enough on the phone.'

With difficulty Wilson left the shade and support of the doorway and, breathing hard, started putting gasoline in the car. In the sunlight his face was green.

'I didn't mean to call you away from your lunch,' he said. 'But I need money pretty bad, and if I could buy your old car, I could make a few dollars on it.'

'What do you want money for, all of a sudden?'

'I want to get away. My wife and I want to go West.'

'Your wife does?' cried Tom in surprise.

'She's going whether she wants to or not. I'm taking her.'

The coupé drove by, with a waving hand at the window.

'Something funny's been going on,' said Wilson. 'I just found out about it in the last two days. That's why I want to get away. That's why I want to buy your car.'

I realized that, so far, he didn't suspect Tom. He had discovered that Myrtle had some sort of life apart from him in another world, and the shock had made him ill. I stared at him and then at Tom, who had made a similar discovery about his own wife less than an hour before.

'I'll send that car over tomorrow afternoon,' said Tom.

The valley of ashes always made me a little uneasy, and now, aware of something threatening behind me, I turned my head. Over the ash-heaps the huge eyes of Doctor T. J. Eckleburg watched as usual, but I soon noticed that other eyes were looking at us with peculiar interest from only a short distance away.

From one of the windows over the garage, Myrtle Wilson was staring down at the car. She wore an expression that I had often seen on women's faces. I realized that her eyes, wide with jealous terror, were fixed not on Tom, but on Jordan Baker – she clearly thought Jordan was his wife.

There is no confusion like the confusion of a simple mind, and as we drove away, Tom was feeling the first waves of terror. His wife and his mistress, until an hour ago safe and

A hot day in town

I soon noticed that other eyes were looking at us with peculiar interest.

protected, were slipping rapidly from his control. He drove faster and faster, with the double purpose of overtaking Daisy and leaving Wilson behind. Soon we were in the city and in sight of the coupé.

'I love New York on summer afternoons when everyone's away,' said Jordan. 'There's something very sensuous about it.'

The word 'sensuous' obviously worried Tom even more. The coupé came to a stop, and we drew up alongside.

'Where are we going?' cried Daisy from the window.

'How about the movies?' suggested Jordan.

'It's so hot!' complained Daisy. 'You go. We'll drive around and meet you afterwards.'

There followed a long, noisy discussion about what to do next. In the end, though we all said it was a crazy idea, we hired a private sitting room in the Plaza Hotel, and that's where we found ourselves half an hour later.

The room was large and hot, and even opening the windows only let in warm air.

'Open another window,' commanded Daisy.

'The thing to do is to forget the heat,' said Tom impatiently. 'You make it ten times worse by complaining about it.'

'Why not leave her alone, old sport?' remarked Gatsby. 'You're the one who wanted to come to town.'

There was a moment of silence.

'That's a great expression of yours, isn't it?' said Tom sharply.

'What is?'

'All this "old sport" business. Where did you pick that up?'

'Now see here, Tom,' said Daisy, 'if you're going to make personal remarks, I won't stay here a minute.'

Suddenly the heat exploded into sound, and we were

listening to Mendelssohn's Wedding March from the wedding taking place in the hotel rooms below us.

'Imagine marrying anybody in this heat!' cried Jordan.

'I was married in the middle of June,' Daisy remembered. 'It was so hot that somebody fainted. Who was it, Tom?'

'A man called Biloxi,' he answered shortly. 'I didn't know him. He was a friend of Daisy's.'

'He was not,' she said. 'He told me he'd been at college with you – he was president of your class at Yale.'

'We didn't *have* any president at Yale,' I said. 'I don't remember him – I don't suppose he ever went there.'

Gatsby's foot beat restlessly on the floor, and Tom eyed him unpleasantly. 'By the way, Mr Gatsby, I understand you're an Oxford man. You must have been there about the time Biloxi went to Yale.'

There was a long pause. This important detail was to be cleared up at last.

'I went there in 1919,' said Gatsby. 'I only stayed five months. That's why I can't really call myself an Oxford man. After the war some of the officers were offered the chance to go to any of the universities in England or France.'

I wanted to get up and shake his hand – I suddenly believed in him all over again. Daisy was smiling now.

'Wait a minute,' said Tom angrily, 'I want to ask Mr Gatsby one more question.'

'Go on,' Gatsby said politely.

'What kind of trouble are you trying to cause in my house?'

They were out in the open at last, and Gatsby was happy.

'He isn't causing any trouble.' Daisy looked desperately from one to the other. '*You* are. Please have a little self-control.'

'Self-control!' repeated Tom. 'I suppose the latest thing is to sit back and let Mr Nobody from Nowhere make love to your wife. Well, if that's the idea, you can count me out!'

'I've got something to tell *you*, old sport—' began Gatsby. But Daisy guessed at his intention.

'Please don't!' she cried helplessly. 'Let's all go home!'

'That's a good idea,' I said, getting up. 'Come on, Tom. Nobody wants a drink.'

'I want to know what Mr Gatsby has to tell me.'

'Your wife doesn't love you,' said Gatsby. 'She's never loved you. She loves me.'

'You must be crazy!' cried Tom automatically.

Gatsby jumped to his feet. 'She never loved you, do you hear? She only married you because I was poor and she was tired of waiting for me. It was a terrible mistake, but in her heart she never loved anyone except me!'

Tom turned to Daisy. 'What's been going on?' he asked.

'I told you what's been going on,' said Gatsby. 'Going on for five years – and you didn't know.'

'You've been seeing this man for five years?' Tom asked Daisy sharply.

'Not seeing,' said Gatsby. 'We couldn't meet. But both of us loved each other all that time, old sport, and you didn't know.'

'I don't know what happened five years ago, before I met Daisy. But the rest of that's a damned lie. Daisy loved me when she married me and she loves me now.'

'No,' Gatsby said, shaking his head.

'The trouble is, she sometimes gets foolish ideas in her head and doesn't know what she's doing. What's more, I love Daisy too. Once in a while I go off and make a fool of myself, but I always come back, and in my heart I love her all the time.'

'You're horrible,' said Daisy. 'So many affairs . . .'

Gatsby walked over and stood beside her. 'Daisy, just tell him the truth – that you never loved him. Then you can forget your life with him for ever.'

She hesitated. Perhaps she realized at last what she was doing, and perhaps she had never intended to go this far. But it was done now. It was too late.

'I never loved him,' she said, with obvious unwillingness.

'Not at Kapiolani?' asked Tom suddenly. 'Not that day I carried you down from the mountain to keep your shoes dry?' There was a clumsy fondness in his voice. 'Daisy?'

'Please don't.' She looked at Gatsby. 'There, Jay,' she said, but her hand was trembling as she tried to light a cigarette. Suddenly she threw the cigarette on the carpet.

'Oh, you want too much!' she cried to Gatsby. 'I love you now – isn't that enough? I can't help what's past.' She began to sob helplessly. 'I did love him once – but I loved you too.'

Gatsby's eyes opened and closed.

'You loved me *too*?' he repeated.

'Even that's a lie,' said Tom fiercely. 'She didn't know you were alive. Why – there're things between Daisy and me that you'll never know, things that neither of us can ever forget.'

The words seemed to bite into Gatsby.

'I want to speak to Daisy alone,' he insisted. 'She's all excited now—'

'Even alone I can't say I never loved Tom,' she said pitifully. 'It wouldn't be true.' She turned to her husband. 'Not that it matters to you,' she added.

'Of course it matters. I'm going to take better care of you from now on.'

'You don't understand,' Gatsby said wildly. 'You're not going to take care of her any more.'

'I'm not?' Tom opened his eyes wide and laughed. He could afford to control himself now. 'Why's that?'

'Daisy's leaving you.'

'She's not leaving me! Certainly not for a damned criminal who'd have to steal the ring he put on her finger!'

'I won't stand this!' cried Daisy. 'Oh, please let's get out!'

'Who are you, anyway?' Tom burst out. 'You're friendly with Meyer Wolfshiem, I know that much.' He turned to us and spoke rapidly. 'I found out that he and Wolfshiem bought up a lot of side-street drug-stores here and in Chicago, and sold grain alcohol to anyone who asked for it – against the law, of course. I thought he was a bootlegger, and I wasn't far wrong.'

'What about it?' said Gatsby politely. 'I guess your friend Walter Chase wasn't too proud to come in on it.'

'And you let him go to jail for it, didn't you? God! You ought to hear what Walter says about *you*!'

'He didn't have a cent when he came to us. He was very glad to pick up some money, old sport.'

'Don't you call me "old sport"!' cried Tom. 'That drug-store business was just small change. I know you've got something on now that Walter's afraid to tell me about.'

I looked at Daisy, who was staring, terrified, at Gatsby and her husband. Then I turned back to Gatsby, and was shocked by his expression. The words of the girl at his party came back to me: *You look at him sometimes when he thinks nobody's looking at him. I'm sure he's killed a man.* For a moment the look on his face could be described in just that fantastic way.

It passed, and he began to talk excitedly to Daisy, trying to persuade her that the accusations against him were not true. But with every word of his, she was drawing further and further into herself, so he stopped that, and only the dead dream fought on as the afternoon slipped away, trying unhappily to reach that lost voice across the room.

The voice begged again to go.

'*Please*, Tom! I can't stand this any more.'

Her frightened eyes told that whatever intentions, whatever determination she had had, were gone forever.

'You two start on home, Daisy,' said Tom. 'In Mr Gatsby's car.' He added scornfully, 'Go on. He won't annoy you. I think he realizes that his arrogant little attempt at an affair is over.'

They were gone, without a word. After a moment or two, we left too. Jordan and I got into the coupé with Tom, and we started for Long Island. Tom was very pleased with himself, talking and laughing all the way, but Jordan and I were not listening. Human sympathy has its limits, and we were happy to let their arguments disappear into the distance, like the lights of the city. I had just remembered it was my thirtieth birthday. Thirty – the promise of years of loneliness ahead of me, a thinning list of single men to know, thinning enthusiasm, thinning hair. But there was Jordan beside me, who, unlike Daisy, was too wise to carry well-forgotten dreams from age to age. As we passed over the dark bridge, her pale face fell lazily against my shoulder, and with her warm hand in mine, the fear of being thirty died away.

So we drove on toward death through the cooling half-light.

•———•

The young Greek, Michaelis, who owned the restaurant beside the ash-heaps, was the main witness at the inquest. At five in the afternoon he had walked over to the garage, and found George Wilson sick in his office – really sick, pale as his own pale hair and shaking all over. Michaelis advised him to go to bed, but Wilson refused, saying he didn't want to lose any business. Suddenly there was violent banging and shouting from upstairs.

'I've got my wife locked in up there,' Wilson explained to his neighbor. 'She's going to stay there till the day after tomorrow. Then we're going to move away.'

Michaelis was extremely surprised, as Wilson had always seemed a very quiet little man, incapable of such behavior. He went back to his restaurant, and didn't come out again until seven o'clock, when he heard Mrs Wilson's voice crying loudly from the garage, 'Beat me! Throw me down and beat me, you dirty little coward!'

A moment later she rushed out into the darkness, waving her hands and shouting. Before he could move, it was all over.

The 'death car', as the newspapers called it, didn't stop. The other car, the one going toward New York, came to rest nearby, and its driver hurried to where Myrtle Wilson, her life violently cut short, lay in the road, her thick dark blood running through the dust. When he and Michaelis tore open her dress, they saw that her left breast was hanging loose, and there was no need to listen for the heart underneath. The great vitality of that warm and living body was no more.

• —— •

We were still some distance away when we saw the three or four cars and the crowd. Tom stopped the car, got out and pushed his way past everybody into the garage. When Jordan and I managed to get inside, we saw Myrtle's body wrapped in a blanket on a work-table, with Tom bending over it. A policeman was writing down names in a little book, and Wilson was holding on to a doorpost with both hands, crying over and over again, 'Oh, my God! Oh, my God! Oh, my God!'

In a few moments Tom was in control of himself again. One

of the witnesses said that the car which hit Myrtle was big, new, and yellowish. Tom was careful to explain to Wilson and the policeman that he himself was driving a coupé, and that the yellow car he had been driving earlier wasn't his.

Leaving Wilson in the care of a couple of men, we got back in Tom's car, and he started driving. In a little while I heard him sob, and saw tears running down his face.

'The damned coward!' he sobbed. 'He didn't even stop!'

Myrtle Wilson rushed out into the darkness, waving her hands and shouting.

At the Buchanans' house there were lights on in an upstairs bedroom. A change had come over Tom, and he spoke seriously and with decision.

'Daisy's home,' he said. 'There's nothing we can do tonight. Nick, I'll phone for a taxi for you. Come in and have some supper with Jordan – if you want any.'

'No, thanks. I'll wait outside for the taxi.'

Jordan put her hand on my arm. 'Won't you come in, Nick? It's only half-past nine.'

I'd had enough of all of them for one day, and suddenly that included Jordan too. She must have seen something of this in my expression, because she turned and ran up the porch steps into the house. I walked slowly away from the front door.

Before I got to the gate, however, I heard my name called, and Gatsby stepped out of the bushes into the path.

'What are you doing?' I asked.

'Just standing here, old sport.' Then he asked, 'Did you see any trouble on the road?'

'Yes.'

He hesitated. 'Was she killed?'

'Yes.'

'I told Daisy I thought so. It's better that the shock should come all at once. She took it very well.' He added, 'I don't think anybody saw us, but of course I can't be sure.'

I disliked him so much by this time that I didn't find it necessary to tell him he was wrong.

'Who was the woman?' he asked.

'Her name was Myrtle Wilson. Her husband owns the garage. How the devil did it happen?'

'Well, I tried to turn the wheel—' He stopped, and suddenly I guessed at the truth.

'Was Daisy driving?'

'Yes,' he said after a moment, 'but of course I'll say I was. You see, when we left New York, she was very nervous and thought she'd feel better if she was driving. Then suddenly this woman rushed out – it seemed to me that she wanted to speak to us. It all happened so fast. I tried to make Daisy stop, but she couldn't. Anyway, I'm going to wait here and see if Tom tries to bother her about that unpleasantness this afternoon. She's locked herself into her room, and if he becomes violent, she's going to turn the light out and on again.'

'He won't touch her,' I said. 'He's not thinking about her.'

'I want to be sure, old sport.'

A new thought came to me. Suppose Tom found out that Daisy had been driving. He might think . . . anything.

'You wait here,' I said. 'I'll see if there's any sign of trouble.'

I walked back to the house, and saw a light in the kitchen. Daisy and Tom were sitting at the table, with a plate of cold chicken between them, and two bottles of beer. He was talking seriously to her, and his hand covered hers on the table. They weren't happy, and neither of them had touched the chicken or the beer, but they weren't unhappy either. There was a closeness about them that looked very natural.

'Is it all quiet up there?' Gatsby asked anxiously when I returned to where I had left him.

'Yes. You'd better come home and get some sleep.'

He shook his head. 'I want to wait till Daisy goes to bed. Good night, old sport.'

He put his hands in his coat pockets and turned back eagerly to watch the house. I felt he did not want me there. So I walked away and left him standing there in the moonlight – watching over nothing.

CHAPTER 8

WILSON'S REVENGE

I couldn't sleep all night. Toward daybreak I heard a taxi go through the gates to Gatsby's house, and immediately I jumped out of bed and began to dress. I felt I had something to tell him, something to warn him about, and morning would be too late.

His front door was still open, and he was standing in the hall, resting against a table, heavy with disappointment or sleep.

'Nothing happened,' he said miserably. 'I waited, and at about four o'clock she came to the window, stood there for a minute, then turned off the light.'

His house had never seemed so enormous to me as it did that night, when we hunted through the great rooms for cigarettes. In the end we found two old, dried-up ones in a box, and, throwing open the garden doors of the sitting room, we sat smoking outside in the darkness.

'You ought to go away,' I said. 'Someone will recognize your car, and tell the police.'

'Go away *now*, old sport? I can't possibly leave Daisy until I know what she's going to do.'

All his secrets were out in the open now, and he would have told me anything, freely, but he wanted to talk about Daisy.

She was the first 'nice' girl he had ever known. He went to her house in Louisville, at first with other officers from his division, and then alone. He had never been in such a beautiful house before. But what gave it an air of breathless loveliness was that Daisy lived there. It excited him, too, that many men had already loved Daisy – it made the prize even more valuable.

But he knew it was an enormous accident that he was in Daisy's house. He might have a wonderful future as Jay Gatsby, but at present he was a penniless young man without a past. So he made the most of his time. He took what he could get, without worrying about the rights and wrongs of it – and finally he took Daisy, one still October night.

He had certainly taken her under false pretences. He let her believe he was from the same social background as her, and that he was fully able to take care of her. But it didn't turn out as he had imagined. He had intended, probably, to take what he could and go – but now he found himself deeply involved. Daisy disappeared into her rich house, into her rich, full life, leaving Gatsby – nothing. He felt married to her, that was all.

When they met again, two days later, it was Gatsby who was unsure of himself, who would do anything to see her again.

• —— •

'I can't tell you how surprised I was to find out I loved her, old sport. And she was in love with me too! Well, there I was, way off my ambitions, getting deeper in love every minute, and suddenly I didn't care. What was the use of doing great things if I could have a better time telling her what I was going to do?'

On the last afternoon before the army sent him abroad, he sat with Daisy in his arms for a long, silent time. Now and then she moved a little, and once he kissed her shining hair. They had never been closer in their month of love than when she brushed wordless lips against the shoulder of his coat, or when he gently touched the ends of her fingers.

• —— •

He did extraordinarily well in the war, and afterwards was sent to Oxford, although he tried very hard to get sent home. Daisy's letters to him were nervous and desperate; she wanted to feel his presence beside her, and to be told she was doing the right thing. She was young, and her little world was full of flowers, dresses, dances, and good-looking men. She wanted her life shaped now, immediately; she couldn't wait. She wanted the decision to be made by some force – of love, of money, of unquestionable reality – that was close to her.

That force took shape with the arrival of Tom Buchanan. His person and his position were healthily large and solid, and Daisy liked this. Doubtless there was a certain hesitation, but also a certain thankfulness that the future had been decided. The letter reached Gatsby while he was still at Oxford.

•——•

The sun had risen now on Long Island, and we went round the house, opening the rest of the downstairs windows. Ghostly birds began to sing among the blue leaves. There was a slow, pleasant movement in the air, promising a cool, lovely day.

'I don't think she ever loved him,' said Gatsby, looking at me challengingly. 'Of course, it's possible that she loved him for just a minute, when they were first married – and loved me more even then, do you see?'

He came back from France when Tom and Daisy were still on their wedding trip, and made a miserable journey to Louisville on the last of his army pay. He stayed there a week, revisiting the places where he and Daisy had been together. He left the town feeling that if he had searched harder, he could have found her. On the train out of town he stretched his arms out of the window, trying to catch a handful of the air that she had breathed. But it was all going by too fast, and he knew he had lost that part of his life, the freshest and the best, forever.

It was nine o'clock when we finished breakfast and went out on the porch. The gardener came to the foot of the steps.

Wilson's revenge

'I'll let the water out of the pool today, Mr Gatsby. Leaves will start falling soon – then there'll be trouble with the pipes.'

'Don't do it today,' Gatsby replied. He turned to me. 'You know, old sport, I've never used that pool all summer?'

I didn't want to go to the city. I knew I wouldn't be able to do any work, but it was more than that – I didn't want to leave him. But finally I stood up. 'I have to go,' I said. 'I'll call you.'

He looked at me anxiously. 'I suppose Daisy'll call too.'

'I suppose so,' I said.

We shook hands and I started to walk away. A little way down the path, I remembered something and turned around.

'They're a rotten crowd,' I shouted across the lawn. 'You're worth the whole damned lot of them.'

I've always been glad I said that. It was the only nice thing I ever said to him. Suddenly his face broke into that wonderful, understanding smile. His pink suit stood out against the white steps, and I thought of the night when I first came to his mansion, three months before. The lawn had been crowded with people who guessed at his crimes – and he had stood on those steps, hiding his unchanging dream as he waved them goodbye.

'Goodbye,' I called. 'I enjoyed breakfast, Gatsby.'

• —— •

Up in the city, I tried to work, but soon fell asleep at my desk. Just before midday the phone woke me, and I jumped nervously out of my chair. It was Jordan Baker. Usually her voice sounded fresh and cool, but today it was hard and dry.

'I've left Daisy's house,' she said. 'I'm going to see some friends in the country this afternoon.'

For some reason it annoyed me that she had left Daisy's.

'You weren't so nice to me last night,' she went on.

'How could it have mattered then?' I replied sharply.

Silence for a moment. Then she said, 'However . . . I want to see you.'

'I want to see you, too.'

'Suppose I change my plans, and come into town this afternoon to meet you?'

'No, it's impossible this afternoon,' I replied, and gave her various reasons.

Then suddenly we weren't talking any more. I don't know which of us put the phone down, but I know I didn't care. I couldn't have talked to her across a tea-table that day, even if it was my last chance to see her in this world.

I called Gatsby's house a few minutes later, but the line was busy. I tried four more times, with no success. Taking out my timetable, I drew a small circle around the 3.50 train. Then I sat back in my chair and tried to think. It was twelve o'clock.

•——•

Now I want to go back a little, and describe what happened at the garage after we left there the night before. Until long after midnight, a curious crowd surrounded the building. In the office, George Wilson sat on a chair, rocking from side to side, his head in his hands. His neighbor, Michaelis, was with him. As the night passed, people went home to bed, and soon the garage was deserted again, except for Wilson and Michaelis.

About three o'clock, Wilson stopped rocking and began to talk about the yellow car. He said he had a way of finding out whom it belonged to. Then he added that a couple of months ago his wife had come from the city with her nose broken.

But when he heard himself say this, he suddenly began to cry, 'Oh, my God!' again. For a moment he was silent. Then a half-knowing, half-confused look came into his pale eyes.

Wilson's revenge

'Look in the drawer there,' he said, pointing to his desk. Michaelis opened the drawer and pulled out a small expensive dog-leash, made of leather, with a silver fastening.

'I found it yesterday,' said Wilson, staring at it. 'She had it wrapped in paper on her dressing-table. I knew there was something funny about it.'

'George, there are plenty of reasons why your wife—'

'Oh, my God!' Wilson broke in. His mouth dropped open suddenly. 'Then he killed her,' he said.

'Who did?'

'It was the man in that car. She ran out to speak to him and he wouldn't stop.'

'It was an accident, George.'

Michaelis believed that Mrs Wilson had been running away from her husband, not trying to stop any particular car.

'Maybe you got some friend that I could telephone for, George?'

He wasn't hopeful. He was almost sure Wilson had no friend – there wasn't enough of him for his wife. He was glad a little later when he noticed the sky getting lighter outside. The night would soon be over.

Wilson's dazed eyes looked out of the window at the ash-heaps. 'I took her to the window,' he said after a long silence, 'and I told her, "God knows everything you've done. You can make a fool out of me, but you can't make a fool out of God!"'

Standing behind him, Michaelis saw with a shock that Wilson was looking at the eyes of Doctor T. J. Eckleburg, which had just appeared, pale and enormous, from the departing night.

'God sees everything,' repeated Wilson.

'That's just an advertisement, George,' Michaelis said kindly.

Wilson's dazed eyes looked out of the window at the ash-heaps.

But Wilson stood there a long time, his face close to the window, staring knowingly into the half-light.

By six o'clock Michaelis was exhausted, and very grateful when another neighbor came to sit with Wilson. Michaelis went home to sleep, and when he hurried back to the garage four hours later, Wilson was gone.

Afterwards it wasn't difficult to discover where he went, at least until midday. There were boys who saw a man 'acting sort of crazy', and motorists at whom he stared oddly from the side of the road. Then for three hours he disappeared from view. The police supposed that he spent that time going from garage to garage, asking about the yellow car. But perhaps he had an easier, surer way of finding out what he wanted to know. By half-past two he was in West Egg, where he asked someone the way to Gatsby's house. So by that time he knew Gatsby's name.

• —— •

At two o'clock Gatsby put on his bathing-suit and told the butler to bring any phone message to him at the pool. He took a rubber mattress that his guests had used during the summer, and walked off among the yellowing trees toward the pool.

No telephone message arrived, but the butler waited for it until four o'clock – until long after there was anyone to give it to if it came. I have an idea that Gatsby himself didn't believe it would come, and perhaps he no longer cared. If that was true, he must have felt that he had lost the old warm world, and paid a high price for living too long with a single dream. He must have looked up through frightening leaves at a new world, full of poor ghosts breathing dreams . . . like that ashen, fantastic figure coming slowly toward him through the trees.

Up at the house, Gatsby's driver heard the shots, but afterwards he only said he didn't think anything much about them. I drove straight from the station to Gatsby's house, and rushed anxiously up the front steps. Supposedly, that was the first thing that alarmed anyone. But the servants knew then, I'm sure of it. Without a word said, four of us – the driver, butler, gardener, and I – hurried down to the pool.

With tiny movements that were only the shadows of waves, the mattress floated irregularly down the pool, carrying its load. A small breath of wind was enough to disturb its accidental journey, and the touch of some leaves on the surface made it turn slowly, leaving a thin red circle in the water.

It was after we started carrying Gatsby toward the house that the gardener saw Wilson's body, a little way off in the grass, and the killing and destruction were complete.

CHAPTER 9

THE FUNERAL

After two years I remember the rest of that day, and that night and the next day, only as an endless routine of police and photographers and newspaper men in and out of Gatsby's front door. A rope stretched across the main gate and a policeman beside it kept out the curious, but little boys soon discovered they could enter through my garden, and there were always a few of them, standing open-mouthed around the pool.

At the inquest, Michaelis mentioned that Wilson suspected his wife of having an affair. But Catherine was determined to protect her sister's good name. She said that Myrtle had been completely happy with her husband, and had not been seeing another man. So it was decided that Wilson had lost his mind as a result of Myrtle's death, and the inquest was closed.

But all this part of it seemed distant and unimportant to me. I found myself on Gatsby's side, and alone. From the moment I telephoned news of the deaths to West Egg village, I was asked to comment on every story about him, and to answer every practical question about him. At first I was surprised and confused; then I began to think that I was responsible, because no one else was interested – interested, I mean, with the deep personal interest of a friend.

I called up Daisy half an hour after we found him, called her without hesitation. But she and Tom had gone away early that afternoon, and taken luggage with them, leaving no address.

I wanted to get somebody for him. I wanted to go into the room where he lay and say confidently, 'I'll get somebody for you, Gatsby. Don't worry.'

Meyer Wolfshiem's name wasn't in the phone book. The butler gave me his office number, but no one answered the phone. I went back to the sitting room, and thought for a moment that all these official people were visitors, friends of his. But, though they drew back the sheet and looked at Gatsby with shocked eyes, his protest continued in my head:

'Look here, old sport, you've got to get somebody for me. You've got to try hard. I can't go through this alone.'

Next morning I sent the butler to New York with a letter to Wolfshiem, which asked him to come out on the next train. That request seemed unnecessary when I wrote it. I was sure he'd start for Long Island when he saw the newspapers, just as I was sure there'd be a wire from Daisy before midday. But neither a wire nor Mr Wolfshiem arrived; no one arrived except more police and photographers and newspaper men. When the butler brought back Wolfshiem's answer, I began to feel scornfully that it was Gatsby and me against them all.

Dear Mr Carraway, This has been one of the most terrible shocks of my life. What a mad thing that man did! It should make us all think. I am involved in some very important business and cannot get mixed up in this now. I am completely knocked out by this.
 Yours truly, Meyer Wolfshiem
P.S. Let me know about the funeral. Do not know his family at all.

When the phone rang that afternoon, I thought it would be Daisy at last. But it was a man's voice, calling from Chicago.

'This is Slagle speaking . . .'

'Yes?' I did not recognize the voice.

'Did you get my wire?'

'There haven't been any wires.'

'Young Parke's in trouble. The police arrested him when he handed over the bonds. Can you believe it?'

'Hello!' I broke in breathlessly. 'Look here – this isn't Mr Gatsby. Mr Gatsby's dead.'

There was a long silence on the other end of the phone . . . then suddenly the connection was broken.

I think it was on the third day that a wire signed Henry C. Gatz arrived from a town in the Mid-West. It said only that the sender was leaving immediately, and asked for the funeral to be put off until he came.

It was Gatsby's father, a serious-looking old man, very helpless and unhappy, wearing a long cheap overcoat in spite of the warm September day. I took him to the room where his son lay, and when he came out, there were tears on his face. He had reached an age where death no longer has the quality of horrific surprise, and when he looked around him now for the first time and saw the large, beautiful rooms of Gatsby's mansion, I could see he was beginning to feel proud as well as sad.

'I didn't know what you'd want, Mr Gatsby—'

'Gatz is my name.'

'Mr Gatz. I thought you might want to take the body West.'

He shook his head. 'Jimmy always liked it better down East. Were you a friend of my boy's, Mr—?'

'We were close friends.'

'He had a big future ahead of him. If he'd lived, he'd have been a great man. He'd have helped build up the country.'

'That's true,' I said uncomfortably. I took him to one of the bedrooms, where he fell asleep at once.

That night an obviously frightened person called up, and demanded to know who I was before he gave his name.

'This is Mr Carraway,' I said.

'Oh!' He sounded calmer. 'This is Klipspringer.'

I was pleased, because that seemed to promise another friend at Gatsby's grave. I'd been calling up a few people, but they were hard to find.

'The funeral's tomorrow. Three o'clock, here at the house. Will you tell anybody who'd be interested?'

'Oh, I will,' he said quickly. 'I'm not likely to see anybody, but if I do, I'll tell them.'

Something in his voice made me suspect him. 'Of course you'll be there yourself.'

'Well, the truth of the matter is, I'm staying with some people up here in Greenwich, and they rather expect me to be with them tomorrow. In fact, there's a sort of party or something. Of course I'll do my best to get away.'

'Huh!' I said scornfully, and he went on nervously, 'What I called up about was a pair of tennis shoes I left there. I'm sort of helpless without them, and I wonder if the butler could send them on. My address is care of B.F.—'

I didn't hear the rest of the name, because I put the phone down.

On the morning of the funeral, it was raining heavily. I went next door, and found Mr Gatz walking up and down excitedly in the hall; he was clearly feeling even prouder of his son's wealth than before. He showed me a photograph of the mansion, torn at the corners and dirty with many hands. Gatsby had sent it to him, and Mr Gatz had shown it so often that I think it was more real to him now than the house itself.

• — •

A little before three o'clock, the minister arrived, and I found myself looking out of the windows for other cars. So did Gatsby's father. And as the time passed and the servants stood waiting in the hall, he looked anxious and spoke of the rain in a worried, uncertain way. I asked the minister to wait for half an hour. But it wasn't any use. Nobody came.

About five o'clock, our three cars reached the cemetery and stopped in heavy rain beside the gate. As we started off on foot toward the grave, I heard another car stop, and looked around. It was the man with owl-eyed glasses whom Jordan and I had found admiring Gatsby's books in the library, three months before. I'd never seen him since then. The rain poured down his thick glasses, and he took them off and dried them, to see the protecting cloth unrolled from Gatsby's grave.

I tried to think about Gatsby then for a moment, but he was already too far away, and I could only remember, without anger, that Daisy hadn't sent a message or a flower.

When it was over, we walked quickly through the rain to the cars. Owl-eyes spoke to me by the gate.

'I couldn't get to the house,' he remarked.

'Neither could anybody else.'

'What!' He looked shocked. 'My God, they used to go there in their hundreds!' He took off his glasses again and cleaned them, outside and in.

'Poor man,' he said.

•——•

I see now that this has been a story of the West, after all. Tom and Gatsby, Daisy and Jordan and I, were all Westerners, and perhaps there was something missing in every one of us, so that we were never able to get used to Eastern life.

After Gatsby's death, I no longer wanted to live in the East – it was full of too many ghosts. So when the blue smoke of dry leaves was in the air and the wind blew the wet clothes stiff on the line, I decided to come back home.

*I could only remember, without anger, that Daisy hadn't sent
a message or a flower.*

The funeral

There was one thing to be done before I left. It was difficult and unpleasant, but I wanted to leave things tidy, and not just hope that the sea would carry my rubbish away. I saw Jordan Baker, and talked over and around what had happened to us together, and what happened afterwards to me.

She lay perfectly still, listening, in a big chair. She was dressed to play golf, and her hair was the color of an autumn leaf. When I had finished, she told me without comment that she was engaged to another man. I doubted that, although there were several she could have married whenever she wanted. For just a minute I wondered if I was making a mistake, then I thought it all over again quickly, and got up to say goodbye.

'You did turn me down, you know,' she said suddenly. 'On the telephone. I don't care at all for you now, but it was a new experience for me, and I felt a little dazed for a while.'

We shook hands.

She went on, 'Oh, and do you remember a conversation we had once about driving a car? You said a bad driver was only safe until she met another bad driver. Well, I met another bad driver, didn't I? It was careless of me to make such a wrong guess. I thought you were rather an honest person. I thought you were secretly proud of that.'

'I'm thirty,' I replied. 'I'm five years too old to lie to myself and call it honesty.'

She didn't answer. Angry, and half in love with her, and enormously sorry, I turned away.

• —— •

One afternoon late in October, I saw Tom Buchanan, walking ahead of me along Fifth Avenue. I slowed up to avoid overtaking him, but he saw me and walked back, holding out his hand.

'What's the matter, Nick? Don't you want to shake hands with me?'

'No. You know what I think of you.'

'You're crazy, Nick.'

'Tom, what did you say to Wilson that afternoon?'

He stared at me without a word, and I knew I had guessed right about those missing hours.

'I told him the truth,' he said. 'He came to our house while we were packing our bags. He was crazy enough to kill me if I hadn't told him who owned the car. What if I *did* tell him? That man threw dust into your eyes just like he did in Daisy's, but he was a tough one. He ran over Myrtle like you'd run over a dog, and never even stopped his car. By God, it was awful!'

There was nothing I could say, except the one thing that was impossible to say – that it wasn't true.

I couldn't forgive him or like him, but I saw that he thought he had good reasons for what he had done. It was all very careless and confused. They were careless people, Tom and Daisy – they smashed up things, and then went back into their money or their huge carelessness, or whatever it was that kept them together, and let other people pick up the pieces . . .

I shook hands with him; it seemed silly not to. Then he went into a jewelry store to buy a pearl necklace or perhaps just some buttons, rid of my small-town moral judgements for ever.

• —— •

Gatsby's house was still empty when I left – the grass on his lawn had grown as long as mine. On the last night, with my cases packed and my car sold, I went over and looked at that huge failure of a house once more. On the white steps a rude word, written by some boy with a piece of brick, stood out clearly in the moonlight, and I rubbed it out, drawing my shoe along the stone. Then I walked down to the beach and lay on the sand.

Most of the big houses along the shore were closed now for the winter, and were in darkness; there was only the shadowy, moving light of a ferryboat across the water. And as the moon rose higher, the houses slowly began to melt away, until I became aware of the old island underneath. Sailors from Holland were the first to set eyes on the island; to them it was a fresh green breast of the new world. For a passing, magical moment, they had the last and greatest of all human dreams, holding their breath in the presence of this new continent, face to face for the last time in history with so great a cause for wonder.

And as I lay there, thinking about the old, unknown world, I thought of Gatsby's wonder when he first saw the green light at the end of Daisy's dock. He had come a long way to this blue lawn, and his dream must have seemed so close to him. He did not know that it was already behind him, somewhere back in the enormous shadows beyond the city, where the dark fields rolled on under the night.

Gatsby believed in the green light, the future that year by year moves further away from us. It escaped us then, but that doesn't matter – tomorrow we will run faster, stretch out our arms further . . . And one fine morning . . .

So we beat on, boats against the current, carried back ceaselessly into the past.

GLOSSARY

admire to like or respect somebody
affair a sexual relationship between two people, usually when one or both of them is married to somebody else
anchor a heavy metal object that is attached to a rope or chain and dropped over the side of a boat, to keep it in one place
arrogance when a person behaves rudely because they feel they are more important than other people
ashes what is left after something has been destroyed by burning
bay a part of the sea partly surrounded by a curve of the land
bond an agreement by a government or company to pay interest on money that people lend them
bootlegger a person who sells alcohol illegally
breasts the two round soft parts at the front of a woman's body
butler the main male servant in a large house
ceaselessly without ever stopping
cemetery an area of land used for burying dead people
champagne an expensive French sparkling white wine
cocktail a drink usually made from a mixture of one or more strong alcoholic drinks and fruit juice
coincidence when two things happen at the same time by chance, in a surprising way
coupé a car with two doors and usually a sloping back
coward a person who is not at all brave
current the movement of water in the sea or a river
damned *(informal)* a swearword used to show annoyance
dazed unable to think clearly, because of a shock
dentist a person whose job is to take care of people's teeth
dock *(AmE)* a raised platform where a boat can be tied up
dog-leash a long piece of leather used for controlling a dog

Glossary

drug-store *(AmE)* a shop that sells medicines and other things
dumb *(informal, AmE)* stupid
embarrassed feeling shy or ashamed
faint to become unconscious because of the heat, a shock, etc.
First Infantry Division the oldest and most famous unit in the American army
formal very correct and polite, not relaxed and friendly
foul extremely bad, dirty, or unpleasant
funeral a ceremony for burying a dead person
gamble to risk money on a card game, horse race, etc.
gas or **gasoline** *(AmE)* a liquid used as fuel in car engines
golf a game played over a large area of grass, using specially shaped sticks to hit a small ball into a series of 9 or 18 holes
grain alcohol an extremely strong alcohol, which is usually not available legally
handkerchief a small piece of material that you use for blowing your nose, etc.
host a person who invites guests to a meal, a party, etc.
inquest an official investigation to find out the cause of somebody's death
joy a feeling of great happiness
lawn an area of ground in a garden, covered in short grass
major a high-ranking officer in the army
mansion a large impressive house
medal a flat piece of metal, which is given to someone who has been brave in war, or who has won a competition
minister a religious leader or a priest
mistress a woman who is having a sexual relationship with a married man she is not married to
moral concerned with principles of right and wrong behaviour
murmur to speak in a soft quiet voice that is difficult to hear
nervous anxious about something that is going to happen

old sport *(old-fashioned)* used as a friendly way of speaking to someone
orchestra a large group of people who play various musical instruments together
owl a bird with large round eyes that hunts at night
porch *(AmE)* a platform with an open front and a roof, built on to the side of a house on the ground floor
power the ability to control people or things; physical strength
represent to be a symbol or an example of something
rock to move backwards and forwards or from side to side
romantic connected with love; emotional and having ideas and hopes that are usually unrealistic
rubber mattress a long thin rubber cushion, containing air, which you can lie on in a swimming pool
scornfully showing, by the way you speak, your strong feeling that somebody or something is not good enough
sensuously in a way that suggests an interest in sexual pleasure
shiver to shake slightly because you are cold, frightened, etc.
slender thin in an attractive or elegant way
smart *(AmE)* intelligent, clever
sob to cry noisily, taking sudden, sharp breaths
sorrow a feeling of great sadness
stand to bear, tolerate, or put up with something
turn out to develop or end in a particular way
unrestful *(adj)* describing people who are never calm or happy or peaceful; Scott Fitzgerald uses it adverbially (**unrestfully**) in *The Great Gatsby*, but the adverb is rare
vitality energy and enthusiasm, being full of life
vulnerable easily hurt physically or emotionally
wire *(AmE)* a message sent from a distant place, using wires that carry electrical signals, then printed and given to somebody
yacht a large sailing boat

ACTIVITIES

Before Reading

1 Read the back cover and the introduction on the first page. What do you know now about the people in the story? Circle Y (Yes) or N (No) for each of these sentences.

1 Jordan Baker is married to Tom. Y/N
2 Nick Carraway is Gatsby's neighbour. Y/N
3 Daisy Buchanan is in love with Nick. Y/N

2 Here are some ideas or phrases which are often connected with F. Scott Fitzgerald and the 1920s. Choose the best words to complete the sentences about them.

1 A bootlegger is someone who . . .
   a) kidnaps people.   b) sells illegal alcohol.
2 The American Dream is . . .
   a) a belief in freedom and equality for everyone.
   b) a guarantee that everyone will become rich.
3 The Jazz Age was a time when . . .
   a) young people started living freer lives.
   b) parents insisted on stricter rules at home.

3 At the beginning of the story, Gatsby is searching for the woman he loves. What do you think will happen in the end? Choose the ending or endings that you would like to happen.

1 Gatsby will find the woman he is in love with.
2 He and she will marry and live happily ever afterwards.
3 She won't love him as much as he loves her.
4 One of them will die, in a tragic misunderstanding.

ACTIVITIES

While Reading

Read Chapters 1 to 4. Complete the paragraph with the names of the right characters. Some names are used more than once.

_____ is in love with _____. Her husband's name is _____, and he has a mistress, _____, who is married to _____. At West Egg, _____ lives next door to _____. He likes _____, a professional golfer, very much; she is a friend of _____'s. In New York, _____ meets a friend of _____'s, a gambler called _____.

Before you read Chapter 5, can you guess what will happen?

1 Nick will invite Daisy to his house for tea.
2 Daisy will refuse to come, and Gatsby will leave West Egg.
3 Gatsby and Daisy will fall madly in love all over again.

Before you read Chapter 7 (*A hot day in town*), choose some of these possible events and guess which characters are involved.

Tom, Nick, Daisy, Gatsby, Jordan, Myrtle, George, Catherine

1 There is an argument.   4 There is a fight.
2 Somebody gets ill.   5 Somebody gets hurt.
3 There is an accident.   6 Somebody is killed.

Before you read Chapters 8 and 9, think about the chapter titles.

1 Chapter 8: *Wilson's Revenge*. Can you guess how Wilson will take his revenge?
2 Chapter 9: *The funeral*. Whose funeral do you think it will be?

ACTIVITIES

After Reading

1 Here are the thoughts of six characters from the story. Who are the characters, who or what are they thinking about, and what is happening in the story at this moment?

   1 'Cool, did she say? Cool? The way she's looking at him! And the look on his face! The rest of us just don't exist. My God, there's something going on between them, I'm sure of it . . .'

   2 'Unbelievable! Just one excuse after another! It's obvious he can't be bothered to see me. Well, that's it. It's over. I thought I liked him, but there are plenty more fish in the sea . . .'

   3 'My darling! I can see where you live, just across the water. Come to me, my love, don't make me wait any longer – I can't stand it! You must have heard of my parties, you must want to see me. I'm here, waiting for you . . .'

   4 'Now, if I bang the lock with my shoe, surely I can break it – yes, I've done it! Quick, down the stairs! He'll be driving back home soon, and the minute I see that yellow car, I'm going to run out in the road and stop him. He *must* take me with him!'

   5 'Three people – his father, the minister, and me. Where are all those people who drank his champagne every weekend? Why aren't they here? We'll have to go – we can't wait any longer . . .'

   6 'That poor man – he's going crazy. What he's saying doesn't make any sense. Not surprising, really. It's not every day your wife gets killed in front of your eyes. I'll come back and check on him later when I've had a few hours' sleep myself.'

ACTIVITIES: *After Reading*

2 Read these conversations between some of the characters, and complete them in your own words.

1 *Daisy and Gatsby, meeting at Nick Carraway's house:*
DAISY: Jay! Is it really you?
GATSBY: Daisy, I've loved you all this time! _____?
DAISY: Of course I do!
GATSBY: But then why on earth _____?
DAISY: I had to marry someone, and you weren't there!

2 *Tom and Daisy, talking in their kitchen after the car accident:*
TOM: We'll say no more about your _____. It's over, do you understand?
DAISY: Yes, Tom.
TOM: We're going to start again, you and I. Shall we pack our bags and _____?
DAISY: All right, Tom, let's do that.

3 *Tom and George, at Tom's house after Myrtle's death:*
TOM: Stop shouting, George! What do you want?
GEORGE: You _____, don't you?
TOM: You mean Gatsby? The man in the yellow car?
GEORGE: That's right. If you don't tell me, I'll _____!
TOM: Don't you dare threaten me! OK, OK, he lives at West Egg. Now are you satisfied?

3 Read these statements by some of the characters, and answer the questions that follow, using your own ideas.

1 *'I am one of the few honest people I have ever known.'*
What do you think this shows us about Nick Carraway's character? Do you agree with his opinion? Why, or why not?

2 *'By God, my ideas may be a little out of date, but I think
  women run around too much these days.'*
  What does this tell us about Tom Buchanan? How does his
  attitude to women affect what happens in the story?
3 *'I'm going to fix everything just the way it was before.'*
  How important was the past to Jay Gatsby? Why was he
  unable to imagine that his plan to get Daisy back might fail?
  What does this show us about his character?
4 *'I hope she'll be a fool – that's the best thing a girl can be in
  this world, a beautiful little fool.'*
  Why did Daisy say this about her new-born daughter? Do you
  agree with her?
5 *'You said a bad driver was only safe until she met another bad
  driver. Well, I met another bad driver, didn't I?'*
  When Jordan Baker said this to Nick, what was she really
  talking about? What was the similarity she saw between Nick
  and herself? Do you think she was right or wrong?

4 **Nick Carraway keeps changing his opinion of Gatsby throughout
  the story. Complete the paragraph about Nick and Gatsby in your
  own words. Use as many words as you like for each gap.**

At Nick's first meeting with Gatsby, he became as curious about
him _____. When Gatsby described his past life, Nick
thought it _____, but when he saw the Montenegro medal
and _____, he believed Gatsby. He became Gatsby's friend,
helped him to _____ for the first time in five years and
to keep their affair _____ Tom. However, when he heard
that Gatsby's car _____, Nick really disliked him. He
stopped being angry with Gatsby when he discovered that Daisy
_____, and after Gatsby's death, Nick felt _____.

ACTIVITIES: *After Reading*

5 **Think about these questions and give your answers.**

   1 Why did Nick's relationship with Jordan Baker fail? Whose fault was it? Could they have been happy together?
   2 What mistakes do you think Gatsby made in his life? Would he and Daisy have had a happy marriage, if they had married when they first fell in love?
   3 Why did Gatsby have so few real friends? Was it because of a weakness in his character, or the result of his difficult early life, or was there some other reason? How did he feel about this?
   4 Should Gatsby have told the police that it was Daisy who was driving when his car hit Myrtle Wilson? Why do you think he didn't tell them?
   5 After Gatsby's death, only Nick and Daisy knew the truth about the accident. Should Nick have told someone? Who should he have told? Why do you think he kept it a secret?

6 **Imagine that Nick Carraway went to the police and told them that it was Daisy who drove the car that killed Myrtle. What do you think happened next? Write a paragraph, giving a new ending to the story. Use any of the ideas below, if you like.**

   - The police believed Nick, and interviewed Daisy.
   - At first Daisy pretended she was innocent.
   - Tom paid the police to forget all about it.
   - Gatsby tried to take the blame.
   - George Wilson committed suicide.
   - Daisy was sent to prison, and Tom divorced her.
   - Nick and Jordan got married.
   - Gatsby waited for Daisy, and married her later.

ABOUT THE AUTHOR

Francis Scott Key Fitzgerald (1896–1940) was born in Saint Paul, Minnesota. His mother adored him, made sure he had the best possible education, and encouraged him to write. His first story was published when he was thirteen. After a short time at Princeton University, he left to join the US Army during World War I, but the war ended before he could take any active part.

In 1918 he met and proposed to the beautiful Zelda Sayre, but she refused him; she had no desire to become the wife of a penniless writer. However, when his first novel, *This Side of Paradise* (1920), became a success, Zelda agreed to marry him. Their relationship was passionate and at times very difficult, but it was the basis for much of Fitzgerald's writing. He once said: 'Sometimes I don't know whether Zelda and I are real or whether we are characters in one of my novels.'

In the 1920s Fitzgerald made several trips to Europe. His second novel, *The Beautiful and the Damned*, was published in 1922 and his third, *The Great Gatsby*, in 1925. He also wrote short stories such as *The Diamond as Big as the Ritz* and *The Curious Case of Benjamin Button*. But it was his novels which made him famous, especially *The Great Gatsby*, now generally considered his finest work. As a detailed portrayal of the Jazz Age (a term invented by Fitzgerald) and a powerful criticism of materialism and 'the American Dream', it has become required reading for most American high school students, and has given enjoyment to generations of readers worldwide.

Inspiration for his work came directly from his own life, his marriage to Zelda, and his observations of contemporary society. He said of *This Side of Paradise*: 'To write it took three months; to conceive it – three minutes; to collect the data in it – all my life.' He was very protective of what he called his 'material', and was furious when Zelda wrote her own semi-autobiographical novel called *Save Me the Waltz* (1932).

Fitzgerald and Zelda had an extravagant lifestyle and were often in financial difficulties. When Zelda's mental health became worse, Fitzgerald had to write film scripts and stories with commercial appeal, in order to pay his wife's medical bills. Eventually they separated; she lived in a mental hospital on the East Coast, while he moved to Hollywood. His fourth novel, *Tender is the Night*, came out in 1934, but he died in 1940, leaving a fifth novel, *The Love of the Last Tycoon*, unfinished.

He died believing himself to be a failure, because he had only had limited financial and critical success in his lifetime. It was not until the 1950s and 1960s that *The Great Gatsby* came to be regarded as one of the best American novels ever written. It has sold in large numbers ever since, and four film versions of it have been made. Scott Fitzgerald is now widely regarded as one of the greatest American writers of the 20th century.

Scott and Zelda are buried in the same grave, and on their gravestone is carved the final sentence from *The Great Gatsby*:

'So we beat on, boats against the current, borne back ceaselessly into the past.'

OXFORD BOOKWORMS LIBRARY

*Classics • Crime & Mystery • Factfiles • Fantasy & Horror
Human Interest • Playscripts • Thriller & Adventure
True Stories • World Stories*

The OXFORD BOOKWORMS LIBRARY provides enjoyable reading in English, with a wide range of classic and modern fiction, non-fiction, and plays. It includes original and adapted texts in seven carefully graded language stages, which take learners from beginner to advanced level. An overview is given on the next pages.

All Stage 1 titles are available as audio recordings, as well as over eighty other titles from Starter to Stage 6. All Starters and many titles at Stages 1 to 4 are specially recommended for younger learners. Every Bookworm is illustrated, and Starters and Factfiles have full-colour illustrations.

The OXFORD BOOKWORMS LIBRARY also offers extensive support. Each book contains an introduction to the story, notes about the author, a glossary, and activities. Additional resources include tests and worksheets, and answers for these and for the activities in the books. There is advice on running a class library, using audio recordings, and the many ways of using Oxford Bookworms in reading programmes. Resource materials are available on the website <www.oup.com/bookworms>.

The *Oxford Bookworms Collection* is a series for advanced learners. It consists of volumes of short stories by well-known authors, both classic and modern. Texts are not abridged or adapted in any way, but carefully selected to be accessible to the advanced student.

You can find details and a full list of titles in the *Oxford Bookworms Library Catalogue* and *Oxford English Language Teaching Catalogues*, and on the website <www.oup.com/bookworms>.

THE OXFORD BOOKWORMS LIBRARY GRADING AND SAMPLE EXTRACTS

STARTER • 250 HEADWORDS
present simple – present continuous – imperative –
can/cannot, must – *going to* (future) – simple gerunds ...

Her phone is ringing – but where is it?

Sally gets out of bed and looks in her bag. No phone. She looks under the bed. No phone. Then she looks behind the door. There is her phone. Sally picks up her phone and answers it. *Sally's Phone*

STAGE 1 • 400 HEADWORDS
... past simple – coordination with *and*, *but*, *or* –
subordination with *before*, *after*, *when*, *because*, *so* ...

I knew him in Persia. He was a famous builder and I worked with him there. For a time I was his friend, but not for long. When he came to Paris, I came after him – I wanted to watch him. He was a very clever, very dangerous man. *The Phantom of the Opera*

STAGE 2 • 700 HEADWORDS
... present perfect – *will* (future) – *(don't) have to*, *must not*, *could* –
comparison of adjectives – simple *if* clauses – past continuous –
tag questions – *ask/tell* + infinitive ...

While I was writing these words in my diary, I decided what to do. I must try to escape. I shall try to get down the wall outside. The window is high above the ground, but I have to try. I shall take some of the gold with me – if I escape, perhaps it will be helpful later. *Dracula*

STAGE 3 • 1000 HEADWORDS

... should, may – present perfect continuous – *used to* – past perfect – causative – relative clauses – indirect statements ...

Of course, it was most important that no one should see Colin, Mary, or Dickon entering the secret garden. So Colin gave orders to the gardeners that they must all keep away from that part of the garden in future. *The Secret Garden*

STAGE 4 • 1400 HEADWORDS

... past perfect continuous – passive (simple forms) – *would* conditional clauses – indirect questions – relatives with *where/when* – gerunds after prepositions/phrases ...

I was glad. Now Hyde could not show his face to the world again. If he did, every honest man in London would be proud to report him to the police. *Dr Jekyll and Mr Hyde*

STAGE 5 • 1800 HEADWORDS

... future continuous – future perfect – passive (modals, continuous forms) – *would have* conditional clauses – modals + perfect infinitive ...

If he had spoken Estella's name, I would have hit him. I was so angry with him, and so depressed about my future, that I could not eat the breakfast. Instead I went straight to the old house. *Great Expectations*

STAGE 6 • 2500 HEADWORDS

... passive (infinitives, gerunds) – advanced modal meanings – clauses of concession, condition

When I stepped up to the piano, I was confident. It was as if I knew that the prodigy side of me really did exist. And when I started to play, I was so caught up in how lovely I looked that I didn't worry how I would sound. *The Joy Luck Club*

BOOKWORMS · CLASSICS · STAGE 5

The Age of Innocence

EDITH WHARTON

Retold by Clare West

Into the narrow social world of New York in the 1870s comes Countess Ellen Olenska, surrounded by shocked whispers about her failed marriage to a rich Polish Count. A woman who leaves her husband can never be accepted in polite society.

Newland Archer is engaged to young May Welland, but the beautiful and mysterious Countess needs his help. He becomes her friend and defender, but friendship with an unhappy, lonely woman is a dangerous path for a young man to follow – especially a young man who is soon to be married.

BOOKWORMS · HUMAN INTEREST · STAGE 5

The Accidental Tourist

ANNE TYLER

Retold by Jennifer Bassett

Everyday life in Baltimore, USA, is full of problems – getting the washing done, buying groceries and dog food, avoiding the neighbors . . . After the death of his son and the departure of his wife, Macon's attempts to run his own life become increasingly desperate – and more and more odd.

Meanwhile, he has to get on with his work, writing tourist guides for business people. Then his dog Edward starts to bite people, and he has to send for Muriel, the dog trainer. And day by day, Macon's life gets more and more complicated.